# The Retreat 2:

## *Men After God's Own Heart*

NOV 2012

# The Retreat 2:

## *Men After God's Own Heart*

Dijorn Moss

URBAN CHRISTIAN

www.urbanchristianonline.com

Urban Books, LLC
78 East Industry Court
Deer Park, NY 11729

The Retreat 2: Men After God's Own Heart Copyright
© 2012 Dijorn Moss

ISBN 13: 978-1-60162-737-7
ISBN 10: 1-60162-737-8

First Printing November 2012
Printed in the United States of America

10 9 8 7 6 5 4 3 2 1

Distributed by Kensington Corp.
Submit Wholesale Orders to:
Kensington Publishing Corp.
C/O Penguin Group (USA) Inc.
Attention: Order Processing
405 Murray Hill Parkway
East Rutherford, NJ 07073-2316
Phone: 1-800-526-0275
Fax: 1-800-227-9604

# The Retreat 2:

## *Men After God's Own Heart*

Dijorn Moss

# Dedication

To my wife, Trinea, you are always there to encourage, strengthen, and love. I love you for all infinity, plus a thousand tomorrows.

To my son, Caleb, my greatest achievement and biggest blessing!

# Acknowledgments

I want to acknowledge the warriors in my life. Some of them have gone on to be with the Lord, and others still remain on the battlefield, fighting the good fight of faith. To my grandfather, Samuel Moss, who left a legacy of knowledge, wisdom, and the pursuit of excellence. To my Uncle Julius, the most unselfish man I have ever known. To my aunt Mary, a woman who is more than a conqueror. To the two toughest women walking the earth, my grandmothers, Doreatha Moss and Ruth Jonice, I love you. To my parents, I love you, and I appreciate our relationships more now that I am a parent and realize the sacrifices parenting entails. I cannot leave out my stepmother, Elainna, and my stepfather, David. I love you guys, and I appreciate the love you show toward me. To my nephews AJ and Airon, I love you boys, and I am proud of you. To my uncle Jeryle, I love you and you're my hero.

To my closest friends, Mike Boykins, Jaton Gunter, Mike Jacques, Shamid Austin, Mike Garrett, and Sean Fritz, I treasure your wisdom, and I value our friendship. To my in-laws, Johnny and Trina Kizzie, thank you for being great parents and raising an amazing woman who I am proud to call my wife. To bestselling author Mary B. Morrison, thank you for your pearls of wisdom and your beautiful nature. Thank you to my fellow Damascus Road authors, as well as my fellow Urban Christian authors. To my editor, Joy, thank you for always seeing the potential of my work and pushing me to become a better writer. To my spiritual leaders, Bishop Noel Jones, Pastor Oscar Dace, and Minister Kevin Murray, truly anointed men of God who have guided me through the various storms of life into manhood.

To every reader, book club, and bookstore that has supported me, thank you. I wanted my writing to have an impact on the masses, and it has, thanks to you. Finally, I want to acknowledge my Lord and Savior Jesus Christ. This book would not have been completed if it weren't for you. I thank you for my gift and purpose, but after all that has transpired in the last two years, I thank you for your grace and mercy. Thank you!

# Chapter One

## *Chauncey*

*Four Weeks until the Men's Retreat . . .*

Chauncey was not sure if online dating was the most Christian way of courtship, but he had met a lovely Christian woman online who seemed to have exactly what he desired in a wife. Therefore, Chauncey found himself at M & M Soul Food on a Friday night. He occupied a table next to the window, which would allow him to spot his date, Regina, when she arrived. She was well versed in the scriptures; she did not watch TV, except for TBN, *All My Children,* and reruns of *Martin.* Finally, and this was not the most important factor, Regina was Foxy Brown fine. He had declared that this year he would find his helpmate and fulfill his God-given purpose of being a minister. Chauncey had concluded that the reason that Pastor Dawkins did not admit him into the ministers' class last year had little to do with him dealing with his brother's death and more to do with the fact that he wasn't married.

Chauncey knew that Pastor Dawkins would not allow another unmarried man to enter his ministers' class. The position of minister was too powerful for a single man to handle, because he would have to offer counsel to a lot of troubled women—beautiful women, young ladies with hourglass frames—and that would open the door for the devil to come in. Lately, Chauncey felt that

Greater Anointing church had been flooded with scandal, and the best way to weather the storm was to bring the leaders back to the principle that it was better to marry than to burn.

An invitation to the ministers' class wasn't the sole reason why Chauncey had decided to date. He longed for companionship. What man would not want to be comforted in the arms of a beautiful woman like Regina? Her photo on the online dating site had a black-and-white background, which only enhanced her glamorous appeal. The Bible was clear when it stated that it was not good for a man to be alone, and while Chauncey enjoyed the company of both his single and married friends, he could not avoid being alone sometimes. He would come home to an empty house every day, and that feeling pricked at his heart.

Chauncey sat nervously inside of M & M Soul Food Restaurant. He had chosen the M & M in Carson because Regina lived in Hawthorne, so the location was neutral for both parties. Chauncey especially liked that the restaurant was right next to the 91 freeway, which would make his drive back to Long Beach much easier. While he waited for Regina to arrive, Chauncey pulled a pocket-sized Bible out of his inside jacket pocket and reviewed some of his highlighted passages in Proverbs.

He focused mainly on the passages that dealt with a virtuous wife and the wisdom that a righteous woman brought to a man. It would be nice if he could bring a date with him to Jamal's wedding. It was 6:45 P.M., and Regina had agreed to meet him at 7:00 P.M. Tardiness was a deal breaker for Chauncey when it came to anything, especially dating. Regina had fifteen minutes.

*Lord, I pray that my date finds her way to the restaurant and that she arrives on time, because I know that your Word declares that we should do things*

*decently and in proper order. That includes show-*
*ing up to dinner on time. I also pray that she will be*
*a respectable woman that will not try to rush things.*
*Above all, that she will be the woman that you would*
*have for me. In Jesus's name I pray. Amen!*

Just as Chauncey concluded his prayer and lifted his head, a woman entered the restaurant. Chauncey wondered what a woman her age was doing out by herself. Only a few streaks of black hair remained on this woman.

"Hello, Deacon McClendon. I'm Regina." Regina extended her hand when she arrived at Chauncey's table.

*No, you're not!* The Regina that Chauncey knew from all those online chats through Christianmate.com was a five-foot-nine-inch mocha cutie-pie. Her profile picture had confirmed that fact.

"God bless you," Chauncey said as he stood up and shook her hand. He shook her hand with both hands because that was how he was raised. He was raised to be a gentleman. He also maneuvered around the table to her side and pulled out a chair for Regina, and the elderly lady sat down.

"Such a gentleman." Regina scanned the restaurant and donned a pleasant smile. "I love this place. Sometimes I come here with my girlfriends from church."

"So do I, um . . . This is somewhat awkward." Chauncey sat down and folded his hands.

"Really? How so?" Regina asked.

"Well, you're not what I expected," Chauncey replied.

"I look just like my picture." Regina tried to strike a pose similar to the one in the picture on her profile.

"Forty years ago, maybe." Chauncey covered his mouth. He did not mean to say what he thought.

"Excuse me?" Regina cocked her head to the side with her hand on her hip.

The horrified look on Regina's face told Chauncey that he had said enough. Awkwardness set in, while the sound of food being fried and tables being bused dominated the atmosphere. The giddy conversations at the neighboring tables helped ease the tension in the room. It was not long before the waitress approached with pen and paper in hand.

"Have you guys decided on what you'll be having?" the waitress asked.

"I just don't know what I want." Regina picked up her menu for the first time and started to scan it.

Chauncey seized the moment to ask the young lady an important question. "Do you, by any chance, have a senior citizen's discount?" Chauncey said, with the menu covering his mouth to muffle his words.

"I'm sorry. We don't," the waitress replied, shaking her head.

The look on Regina's face indicated that Chauncey had been unsuccessful in his attempt to hide what he and the waitress were talking about.

"I'll have the liver and onions." Regina closed the menu.

"I'll have the fried chicken dinner with greens, mac and cheese, and corn bread," Chauncey said. He did not take his eyes off of Regina.

The waitress collected the menus and made her way to the kitchen. Moments later she came back to drop off two glasses of water.

"So I'm not what you expected?" Regina said before she took a sip of her water.

"It's not that. It's just that I wonder how long ago it was when you took that profile picture."

"Why does it matter?"

"It matters because I thought that I was going to meet a woman my age."

Regina's online dating profile said she was ninety-nine. That was not anything new. Most women put ninety-nine as their age for their online profiles. Chauncey took it as a polite way of saying, "It's none of your business how old I am!" But as he sat across from his date, he wondered if Regina was literally ninety-nine.

"Why? How old are you?" Regina asked.

"Thirty-eight," Chauncey replied. "How old are you?"

"Didn't your mother ever teach you that it's rude to ask a woman her age?" Regina cocked her head to the side in disbelief.

"Here you guys go." The waitress came over with two hot plates in her hands. She sat the plates down.

"It's also rude for a woman to lie about her age, and it's a sin." Chauncey grabbed his corn bread, broke it in half, and started to eat after a brief moment. He promised to repent later for not praying.

"Are you kidding me? I can't believe this is how you really are," Regina said.

"You know that I'm about walking the narrow path of righteousness. I've been up front and honest, unlike some people at this table."

"Yeah, that's not the only thing that is narrow about you. I believe age is only a number, and you're as young as you feel."

"Did you get that from a Cracker Jack box? I'm serious. How silly is that? Age in this country means everything, from getting your license to being able to vote to being able to run for president. It also means being able to cash a Social Security check and go play bingo at an Indian casino."

Regina must've read the expression on Chauncey's face, because she put her head down and ate some of her food before she spoke again. "I'm sixty!"

Chauncey swallowed hard and waited for his throat to clear before he proceeded. "Excuse me? Sixty? I must not have heard you correctly. You must've said forty."

"Yes, sixty. Six zero. It's hard to find a good man my age." Regina shrugged her shoulders and took a bite of her liver and onions.

*Much less an alive one,* Chauncey thought to himself. The devil was truly a liar, and he was ugly. He had infiltrated the online dating scene and had caused perversion to come into the heart of this vulnerable old woman.

"Why the deception?" Chauncey asked.

"I wasn't being deceptive. That picture on my profile is me."

"From a very long time ago," Chauncey added.

"Do you base things off of looks?" Regina asked.

"No, I base things on whether or not I have to pick you up from your home or from a convalescent home."

Just then, Regina flung a heap of food into Chauncey's face. The juice from the onion-littered gravy stung Chauncey in the eyes, and he could not see out of one eye.

"You're the most disrespectful man I know," Regina said as she got up and stormed out of the restaurant.

"That says a lot, considering you were probably there at the Last Supper," Chauncey shouted with one eye open.

Chauncey was humiliated. He could hear the snickers coming from some of the patrons in the restaurant. He had half a mind to call the police on her, but who would take him, a man assaulted by liver and onions, seriously.

# Chapter Two

## *Will*

*Three Weeks until the Men's Retreat . . .*

Will thought of a lot better places to die than in the middle of his parents' living room. For the third time in his life, Will felt the edge of his father's .380-pistol pressed against his forehead. That equaled the amount of hugs Will had received from his father, and that surpassed the amount of kisses by three. There were two things Odell did not tolerate: weakness and disrespect. The two previous times Will's father had put a gun to his head was to drive out weakness. Tonight was for a lack of respect shown by Will. Tonight Odell planned to teach his oldest son a lesson right in front of the whole family.

"Whew. Look at those eyes, ice cold. Not even Jesus could change that." Odell let a grin sneak out from his poker face.

Will knew his father wouldn't pull the trigger. His father was a disturbed individual, but even Odell was not sadistic enough to kill Will in front of his mother and baby sister. Twenty years of life had taught him how to react to his father's empty threats. This was a test to see who, between Jesus and Odell, had the most influence over him. Will couldn't look rattled, and he couldn't show fear.

"Go ahead. Pull the trigger." Will eyes did not betray him.

"Do you hear that, Josh? That's how a punk talks. That's how a little boy talks. That's the sound of weakness," Odell said to his youngest son, who sat at the table with an ice pack over his face and fear in his eyes.

"I don't need a gun to prove I'm powerful," Will replied.

Odell's smile evaporated, and Will braced for impact. His father could never handle an intellectual debate. Odell always punctuated his arguments with his fists. A chill swept over Will at the horrors that awaited his baby sister, Elisha.

"Man, you ain't going to keep using my brother as a punching bag, neither. I promise you that." Will balled up his fists as tightly as he could, prepared to strike.

"It's nothing, bro. It's whatever. I got out of line, and I'm straight now," Joshua said.

Will had given his life over to Christ a year ago and had moved out of his parents' place as a result. In that short time, Odell had managed to initiate Will's brother Joshua into the family business of stealing cars. Will had sat in that same chair five years ago with an ice pack over his cheek, grateful that his father had taught him how to be a man and how to conquer the streets. Will didn't remember what he had done back then to cause Odell to teach him a lesson with his fists. In time, Joshua wouldn't remember what he had done, either, to take a beating from their father. Will knew his influence over Joshua had diminished.

A tear progressed down Will's bronze cheek, and rage overcame his father. The tear caused more damage than the threat. Odell removed the gun from Will's forehead and tucked it behind his back, into his pants. Odell hesitated for a moment before he gave Will a two-handed shove.

"Dad!" Joshua jumped up from his seat and dropped the ice pack. He made a move toward Odell but froze when Will regained his balance. Will did not need his little brother to fight his battles.

Odell had gotten weaker and slower since his release from prison. Will remembered when his father could push him from one side of the room to the other. Odell also had a right hand like a heavyweight boxer, but Will barely moved after his father's push. Odell left the right side of his chin open for an attack. Will was faster than his father remembered and could get in two punches before Odell even knew what hit him. One thing kept the surge of emotions that rumbled inside of Will at bay, and that was his faith. Which strength packed more power? Will's physical strength or his spiritual awakening? Will chose the latter and unballed his fists.

Will looked over his father's shoulder and spotted his mother's enlarged eyes as she observed the altercation. Before the argument turned physical, Will's mother pretended to be transfixed by an episode of *Good Times*. Carroll, Will's mother, usually stayed in such a drug-induced haze that Odell could fire a rocket launcher at Will and she would not even notice nor care.

Even if for once his mother was not under the influence of drugs, Carroll remained too mentally broken and emotionally bankrupt to broker a peace deal between her husband and son. She stayed high so that she did not have to face her reality.

"What kind of mother would sit there and let her husband put a gun to her son's head? Let him beat on her youngest son and push the oldest without saying a word?" Will muttered. He refused to let his mother off the hook. Her silence was a greater offense than Odell's actions.

"She ain't got to do nothing but just sit there and watch TV, because I got this." Odell pounded his chest.

Carroll said it all when she turned away from Will and resumed watching her program. She did not utter a word, and Will's heart had an ache that accompanied each beat.

"Wow, I took care of this family when Dad was locked up, and you would rather him kill me than for once be a mother and protect your children?" Will remarked.

"She's the reason why you're so weak. All she did was spoil you and your brother," Odell said.

"Really? When did she spoil me or my brother? When she left me alone in the house when I was five for a whole day? When she bought me a bunch of toys for Christmas and turned around and sold them for drugs two days later? And where were you?"

"I was playing my hand. Everything you are now and everything you believe in was given to you by the white man. I ain't saying what I did was right, but I didn't have a choice in the matter, now did I?"

"We all got a choice, and you should let Joshua decide who he wants to be with," Will said.

"Joshua, get over here!" Odell's eyes did not move away from Will.

Without hesitation, Joshua made his way over to his father and brother.

"Josh, tell your brother that you don't want to go anywhere," Odell said to Will's baby brother.

"Bro, I miss you being here. I wish you were here and that we were a family again." Joshua's voice cracked under the weight of his words.

"Oh yeah? Let's be a family again. Let's let Pop use us as punching bags while Mom shoots up. Let's all go on a lick together and get caught by the pos, and when Elisha is out of her training bra, let's put her on the pole and make our family complete. One big dysfunctional family."

Will could not harbor any ill feelings toward his brother. Joshua was scared, and Will wished Joshua could see that there was another way.

"You know I can't, Josh. I'm trying to get my life together, and I can't live like this anymore."

"Then go. Bounce!" Odell gestured for Will to leave.

"Please, bro. I need you here," Joshua said.

"I'm always going to be here for you, Josh. Just call me if you need me." Will gave his brother a hug, and fear transferred from Joshua to Will. "I love you, Josh. Stay up."

Joshua did not say anything, and Will remembered another one of his father's creeds: the word *love* was said by women and sissies. Love did not have to be said if it was shown.

Will broke from Joshua's embrace and sidestepped his father, who looked too annoyed to say anything. He walked over to his baby sister Elisha's crib. Positioned next to the flat-screen TV on the opposite side from where his mom sat on the couch, Elisha lay sound asleep. None of the family's melodrama disturbed her slumber. Will leaned in and planted a kiss on her forehead.

Will then walked over and kissed his mother on the cheek. The kiss he gave his mother was not the same as the one he gave Elisha. Elisha's kiss was spawned out of the love Will had for his baby sister. Will kissed his mother out of habit. Once again Carroll remained passive when Will needed her to play an active role in his life.

"Bye, Mom," Will said before he slid between Joshua and his father.

"Don't ever, so long as you live, think that you can come up in here and tell me how to raise my seed. You hear me!" Odell said.

Will did not break his stride as he headed for the door. Before he opened the door, he took one last look back at his dysfunctional family portrait. Will then opened the door and closed it in a swift motion.

Once outside, Will tried to recall everything that had just transpired. He wanted to call child protective services, but a judge shouldn't have to decide on family matters. Will wanted Joshua to stay with him, and Joshua wanted Will to move back home. If Will's life was a game of chess, then he and his brother had just reached a stalemate.

As Will walked along the second-floor balcony, he noticed that a former member of his gang, the Untouchables, stood in the parking lot, next to a red Honda Accord. D-Loc had vowed to get even after Will turned his back on his set to follow God. Every time Will came anywhere near his father's place, he was in danger, so he had to minimize his visits and make sure to leave before anyone noticed. It was easy to do with a black and silver Ninja ZX-10R, a gift from a fellow church member, Quincy, and it came in handy in tight situations. The question now, however, was, would Will make it to his bike before his old comrade called in reinforcements?

# Chapter Three

## *Titus*

"*I won't be needing this anymore.*" Pastor Lemont Dawkins handed his black leather-bound Bible to his son, Titus.

Despite his reluctance, Titus accepted his father's Bible. Titus also accepted that his father no longer loved his mother and that Lemont Dawkins would leave the confines of his family for the love of another woman. Lemont packed his bags and placed them by the front door. Titus was all that stood between him and the front door.

In Titus's worldview, his father was one sermon short of being a god. Titus often repented for his idol worship of his father, but he could not find fault in either his father or his pastor. Pastor Lemont Dawkins's sermons served as a stain remover to the wearied sinner. He embodied charisma and conviction, but the man who Titus wanted to be like was only a fraction of the man Lemont truly was. There were sides of Titus's father that played out only within the sanctity of the master bedroom.

"I have no more use for that book, and its lies," Lemont declared , referring to his Bible, which was now in Titus's hands.

"That's just the devil talking. Don't give in to his lies, Daddy." Titus fought back the tears. At fifteen, he pos-

*sessed a firm grasp on the obvious: the family in the portraits and pictures and on the bulletin boards was not the family that dwelled in this postmodern three-bedroom flat.*

*His father had kept a lot of secrets, and Titus could no longer turn a deaf ear to the murmurs or a blind eye to the evidence.*

*"You're talking to the devil right now." Victoria, Titus's mother, emerged from the master bedroom with a handful of collared shirts, which she did not hesitate to throw at Lemont in her effort to aid him in his departure. Lemont used his forearm to defend against the assault from his wardrobe, courtesy of his wife. Victoria had already arrived at a place that Titus still grappled with, that he might not ever see his father again after this night.*

*"You're a mighty fine one to talk. You never accepted the fact that I'm a man and I have needs." Lemont picked up his clothes from the floor and draped them over his arm.*

*"I was a good wife to you. I followed the scriptures, and if that's not enough for you, then I know it'll be more than enough for the next man." Victoria stormed back into the master bedroom and slammed the door.*

*Titus knew that his mother had retreated to her room because she would not give his father the satisfaction of seeing her cry. His mother was often criticized throughout the church for her rock-like nature. It did not seem ladylike in a traditional church for a woman to carry the rigidness of a man. What most people misunderstood about Victoria, Titus knew perfectly well. He compared his mother's nature to that of a solid rock. She had to endure the scorn and shame that accompanied being the pastor's wife. Titus mother's greatest affliction was being in love with a fool.*

"Dad, you can't turn your back on God and your family like this!"

"Son, I've come to the conclusion that God has turned His back on me. I've tried. I've fasted, prayed, and poured over the scriptures, and nothing. No deliverance, no breakthrough. Do you know how hard it is to watch people get delivered, while you remain a slave? This desire in me doesn't let up. I didn't even want to get married, but your granddaddy and the church forced us to and told us that it's better to marry than to burn. Well, I'm through taking God's advice and the church's advice."

Titus had heard the rumors, but it was in his nature not to listen to them. Titus stayed focused on getting closer to God and his promising basketball future. Titus stood six foot three inches tall. The whole town was ecstatic about his future. There was not a corner in the church Titus could go to where he was not confronted by a mother of the church and her daughter. Even fathers who were vehemently opposed to their daughters dating did not mind if their daughter dated a well-mannered preacher's kid with a formidable jump shot.

"Do yourself a favor, son, and don't become a preacher. That pulpit and that book"—Lemont pointed at the Bible he had just given Titus—"have destroyed the men in this family."

Bishop Samuel Dawkins, Titus's grandfather, had for years carried on an affair, which his grandmother had accepted.

She harked back to a time when folks did not get a divorce, because it was a sin, and so Titus's grandmother tolerated her husband's infidelity for the sake of her salvation. Titus's mother was not that way. She would rather be alone and happy than married and miserable.

*"Dad, don't do this!" Titus clasped his hands together as if to pray.*

*"As far as I'm concerned, I don't owe nobody nothing! I don't want forgiveness, neither, except from you. I hope you can forgive me for what I've done. And take my advice. If you want to be happy, then stay away from that pulpit." Lemont made his way toward the door.*

*"No, Dad!" Titus tried to impede his father's progress, but a punch to the solar plexus brought a swift end to Titus's campaign.*

*"I'm sorry," Lemont said in a tone that lacked compassion.*

*Those were Lemont's last words. Once the pain subsided, Titus went into his mother's bedroom. While she pretended not to cry, her face told a different story. Titus did not know what to say. In truth he had borne witness to something a fifteen-year-old should not have to experience, the self-destruction of a first family.*

Titus was pulled out of his sleep by the sound of the television, which meant one thing: Grace had fallen asleep with the television on again. Titus got up and walked around to Grace's side of the bed, where he always found the remote.

This act repeated itself every night, and whether it was a bad dream or the sound of the TV, Titus Dawkins knew that he would not be able to go back to sleep for the rest of the night. The clock showed 4:15 A.M., and Titus was amazed that he had even gotten fifteen more minutes of sleep than resulted from his usual routine of in bed by midnight and up by four.

Grace, on the other hand was sound, asleep. For Pastor Titus Dawkins, how a person slept told him all he needed to know to determine whether that person was at peace or having a conflict. Grace didn't mistreat people, she didn't harbor bitterness or unforgiveness in her heart, and as a result, Grace slept with a head light of affliction. Titus, on the other hand, wrestled with his past and operated off of minimal sleep.

Titus slipped out of his bedroom and walked down the steel spiral staircase. Titus had two offices, one at the church and another in his three-bedroom condo with an ocean view. But neither could compare to Titus's kitchen table. The two offices were more like storage facilities than a place for studying. With the rapidly changing times, the paper and pen had become ancient tools of the past. Titus now composed both his sermons and his notes on his iPad.

Titus wanted to start a series on King David and focus on why God said he was a man after his own heart when it was clear that David was deeply flawed. How did a flawed person win God's heart? Through the years, Titus had preached on the story of David backward and forward. To have a deeper understanding of the text and bring new revelations was what separated Titus from other pastors.

Success also separated Titus from his predecessors. His driveway had a BMW 7 Series and a Range Rover. Titus enjoyed his success, which most men in his family had never achieved. The demons that chased the Dawkins men generally left them with a divided home, a lost congregation, and a broken pulpit. Titus lived in fear of his lineage every moment.

He was not tormented by the sins of his father, but by the temptations. Titus was always cognizant of the fact that a fall from the top was usually the hardest to overcome. He did not listen to his father's advice. Titus followed the call God had placed on his life, and for better or worse, he had no regrets.

Titus suffered from sleep deprivation, but he did not suffer from a lack of purpose. He spent a few minutes at the table in prayer before he went to the refrigerator to take out a protein shake that he had made the night before. After he retrieved his nutritional beverage, Titus returned to his kitchen table. Titus powered on his iPad and started to thumb through his sermon notes. At around 6:30 A.M., his staff would show up to get him prepared for the eight o'clock service.

"You can't sleep again, I see," Grace said.

"Yeah, I'm just trying to put the finishing touches on this message for the prayer breakfast."

"Uh-huh." Grace took Pastor Dawkins by the hand and fixed his wedding band so that the small diamonds of his platinum ring faced up.

"You're a messenger of God, and we know that God watches over His Word, and He'll put the finishing touches to your messages while you come back to bed and put the finishing touches on me." Grace's eyes changed from nurturing to alluring.

"Now, you know my staff will be here soon. I get to fooling around with you, and I may have to have Pastor Ford preach again."

"And that's the last thing that I need, for your staff to look at me and think I'm crazy for having you miss another service," Grace said.

"How about some breakfast?" Titus asked.

"I'd like that very much."

Titus was making his way to the refrigerator when the phone rang and stopped him dead in his tracks.

"I'll get it." Grace got up and grabbed the cordless on the counter. "Good morning? Hello? Hello?" Grace hung up the phone after a few seconds of trying to get the caller to speak. "That's strange."

"Indeed," Titus said.

Titus went into the refrigerator and removed half of a cantaloupe. He placed the cantaloupe on a counter and removed a butcher's knife from its iron home. Titus sawed a circle around the cantaloupe before he removed a middle chunk. He then grabbed a paper towel and placed it next to the cantaloupe. He began to scrape the seeds from his cantaloupe chunk onto the paper towel. All the while, Grace's eyes held amazement. Titus knew that it was a two-way street when it came to a woman's heart. Men who could not only appreciate a good meal, but could also prepare one were a rarity. Titus went back into the refrigerator and removed vanilla yogurt, granola, and raspberries. He filled the hole he'd made in the cantaloupe with the yogurt first, then the granola, before he topped it with the raspberries.

"Here you go, beautiful." Titus served the cantaloupe on a plate to Grace and handed her a spoon.

"It's a crime to be that anointed, that fine, and know your way around the kitchen."

"I consider myself a very blessed man," Titus said.

"So I've been thinking about your problems with sleeping," Grace said before she took a bite.

"Oh, and what's your prognosis, Doc?" Titus took a seat next to his wife.

"Maybe you should talk to someone."

"The pastor of a thriving ministry seeing a shrink?"

"Don't be prideful."

"Honey, it's not about being prideful. I just believe that my problem is spiritual and it's affecting my psychological state."

"You almost made me cuss, because you know that sleep deprivation *is* a psychological problem. If it was only spiritual, then the pastor of a thriving ministry would've driven it out by now."

Titus mustered up only a chuckle for a retort. His wife was sharp, and she did not mince words.

"Baby, I'm just saying that I worry about you burning yourself out. I don't know how you did this for so long before I came on the scene," Grace said. "God has empowered me to carry out the purpose He's placed in my life. God has empowered me to tell you when to sit still and rest. I want to be able to wake up next to my husband and make breakfast for him for a change."

"That would be nice," Titus replied.

Titus and Grace embraced silence and their food. Today Titus would preach the 8:00 A.M. and 11:00 A.M. service at Greater Anointing and would travel to Riverside to preach at Open Doors Community Church in the evening. He savored his last few minutes of silence.

"Have you called your mother?" Grace asked between bites.

"No, not lately. I've been meaning to call her."

"Her birthday is next week," Grace replied.

"I know when my mother's birthday is." Titus paused a moment to check his tone. "I'll send her a dozen Casa Blancas, along with some cash, as I always do."

Grace did not respond immediately, and Titus was relieved that the conversation appeared to be over.

But Grace went on. "We should take her out. Get her away from that nursing home for a little while."

"I don't think that's a good idea," Titus replied, finishing his breakfast.

"You're still mad about the wedding, aren't you?" Grace pushed the cantaloupe away from her.

Titus slid the cantaloupe into the trash can under the sink and placed the plate and spoon in the sink without making eye contact with his wife. "I told you not to send her an invitation. That was a waste of time."

"What mother wouldn't want to come to her only child's wedding?" Grace asked.

"One who doesn't approve of her son getting married. One who doesn't approve of any decision her son has made since God called him to be a pastor."

"You're not your father," Grace replied.

"My mother remains unconvinced," Titus said.

"Life is short, and you're all that your mother has." Grace pulled Titus by the chin and gave him a kiss. "Just tell me you'll consider it."

"With you seducing me like this, I'll consider anything." Titus gave Grace another kiss, and the taste of Grace's lips lingered.

The doorbell rang. Titus and Grace gently bumped their heads together.

"I'll get that." Grace broke away and went toward the front door.

With Grace, Pastor Dawkins knew pleasure, companionship, wisdom and, above all, love. He and Grace shared a love that was so powerful and yet so delicate that Titus could not have a prolonged engagement. Titus and Grace were married last August, exactly ten months from the day they first met at the men's retreat, of all places. While their intention was to have a private ceremony with only immediate family and close friends present, the celebration of the two taking their vows grew into a spectacle. Titus was happy, but he wondered if his father's words would finally come to fruition.

"Good morning, Pastor." Janice, Titus's personal assistant, entered the kitchen with iPad in hand.

"Good morning, Janice." Titus started to put away the remains of his protein shake.

"You are preaching today, right?" Janice asked.

"Yes." Titus let out a chuckle because over the years he had been a pulpit dictator and had hardly ever allowed anyone to guest speak on Sundays. Since his

marriage to Grace, Titus had been a lot more generous
with his pulpit and had even taken a couple Sundays
off to spend with his new wife.

"Hey, Pastor. How are you?" Reggie, Titus's armor
bearer, entered the room.

"I'm good, Doc. I got my iPad, which I need to put in
my briefcase, I have to grab a quick shower, and I'll be
ready to go." Titus made his way to the kitchen table,
but Reggie beat him to it and packed up Titus's iPad.

"I got this, Pastor," Reggie said.

"Thanks, Doc. I just need to hop in the shower. I'll be
ready in fifteen."

"Hey, hey now." Carlos, Titus's driver, entered behind Grace.

"Carlos! I just need fifteen minutes. Here you go."
Titus grabbed the keys to his Range Rover and tossed
them to Carlos.

"I'll pull the truck around the front," Carlos replied.

"Okay. I'll be ready in a minute," Titus said to his
staff and his wife. He shot upstairs and made his way
into his master bathroom, where he had a shower with
three showerheads. Titus relaxed under the warm
pressure of the water and could feel the muck of yesterday washing away.

"Mind if I join you?" Titus had not heard the door
open, but there was Grace, clothed in nothing but a
glow. At that moment, Titus knew that his staff would
have to wait twenty minutes before he came down.

# Chapter Four

## Quincy

*Two Weeks until the Men's Retreat . . .*

"And when I get that feeling, I want sexual healing."
Quincy danced like he was one of the lost members of
the Temptations. Complete with a spin and a slide.

His wife, Karen, had worked late for the last two
Fridays, and tonight Quincy had a spirit of spontane-
ity. He filled their Jacuzzi bathtub with rose petals.
Chocolate-covered strawberries chilled in the Sub-
Zero refrigerator, alongside a bottle of Chianti. A rich
four-cheese lasagna sat on the stove. Quincy checked
himself out in front of his mirror. He could not decide
whether or not to unbutton two or three buttons on his
shirt. The three buttons open carried more sex appeal,
but the hair on Quincy's chest was less appealing. He
ran into the bathroom and grabbed his razor. Quincy
shaved the excess hair on his chest and went back to
the mirror. Now he looked much better.

The garage door opened, and Quincy made his way
down the stairs and into the hallway next to the door
to the garage. He leaned against the wall and put his
hands in his pockets, simply because it was cool. The
door opened, and Karen emerged. She walked in with
briefcase and purse in hand.

"Hello, Mrs. Page," Quincy said in his deepest, sexi-
est voice without coming off corny.

Karen dropped her bags and rushed over to Quincy. She hopped on him and wrapped her legs around him and started to kiss him.

"I made dinner. Well, I didn't *make* dinner. I actually ordered—"

"Don't say another word. I just want you to take me upstairs and make love to me until I forget all about my long day."

Quincy didn't say another word. He maneuvered Karen over his shoulders and carried her upstairs. Quincy knew that Karen loved when he threw her over his shoulders like Tarzan. It made her squeal, while it made Quincy's back hurt.

Two hours later, Quincy and Karen ate chocolate-covered strawberries on their granite kitchen counter. Karen now wore Quincy's collared shirt, and Quincy had on his black tank top and his boxer shorts.

"That's exactly what I needed." Karen bit into a strawberry.

"Yeah, you wore me out," Quincy replied. They kissed and fed each other the chocolate-covered strawberries and wiped the excess chocolate off of each other's mouths with their fingertips. "I was thinking that maybe we should get away this weekend. Let's go to Palm Springs and stay at the Parker."

Karen wiped the chocolate from her mouth. "I have a ton of work to do."

"So do I, but you're more important. I just don't want us to get so caught up in other things that we miss what's important."

The Lord had proved to be a miracle worker when it came to Quincy and Karen's marriage. A year ago Quincy would have never imagined that he and Karen could survive an affair, but God had pulled them from the muck of infidelity. Now their passion for each other burned stronger than ever. Prayer and a lot of therapy were the tools that he and Karen had used to rebuild. He was mindful about what he said to Karen. Quincy made sure not to say anything out of malice in an argument. Quincy did not act like his and Karen's affairs never took place; he just accepted that his and Karen's actions were moments of weakness.

"Can I ask you something?" Karen asked.

"Sure," Quincy said.

"Do you think our love for each other has grown?"

"I don't know if it has grown, as opposed to us rediscovering what has always been there. I never stopped loving you. I just think that we stayed in one season too long and got comfortable."

"I just wonder what would've happened if we had had more nights like this," Karen said.

"Sasha would've had a brother or sister."

"I'm not talking about the sex, silly. I'm talking about the intimacy that we are sharing here and now. What would've happened?"

"That's a waste of energy playing the what-ifs. I've had plenty of buildings where I wondered what would've been the outcome if I had designed it a different way or built it differently. Then I realized there's nothing I can do. The building has been built. All I can do is take both the success and the miscalculations on to the next building."

Karen took another bite into her strawberry and wiped the chocolate from her lips. Quincy stole a kiss from her, and the taste of her lips blended with chocolate gratified his desire.

"We can't change how we built the first twenty years of our marriage. But we can change how we build the next twenty. We can start by a getaway out of the city for the weekend," Quincy said.

"Okay. Let's go!" Karen said as she wrapped her arms around Quincy's neck and kissed him. Quincy picked Karen up and sat her on the counter. It was time for round two.

The next day Quincy whistled as he placed his golf clubs in the back of his new Porsche Cayenne. He planned to hit a few balls, make a little love, and eat overpriced crab cakes. Karen came out in a sundress with her sunshades and a smile. Quincy was afraid that they might not even make it to Palm Springs, with his wife looking so good.

"Looking very good, Mrs. Page," Quincy complimented.

"You're looking pretty hot yourself," Karen replied.

They kissed again, and this time when they broke free, Karen gave Quincy a pat on the behind.

"Watch out, now." Quincy said, then opened the passenger side door and helped his wife into her seat. He was making his way toward the driver's seat when Sasha's cranberry Lexus IS 300 pulled up in front of his driveway. Sasha, his daughter, hopped out of the car.

"Hey, Dad!"

"Sasha, what are you doing here?" Quincy asked.

Karen hopped out of the car and took off her sunshades. "Baby, why are you here?"

"I just missed you guys and wanted to come home." Sasha gave her mother a hug. "Were you guys heading somewhere?"

"Yes, we were about to go out of town for the weekend," Karen replied.

"Oh, well, I was just wondering if I could stay here for the weekend. I don't want to bother you guys. I just need some time to myself," Sasha said.

"Of course you can stay. I'm just confused as to why you're down here," Karen said.

"She's not the only one," Quincy said as he made his way around the car to observe his daughter.

"I'll tell you all about it when you get back," Sasha said.

"No. Tell us now so that whatever it is we need to straighten out, we can do that." Quincy pointed to the front door, and Sasha made her way into the house.

Quincy and Karen followed her into the house, and Quincy closed the door behind him.

"I'm confused. It's September. There isn't a major holiday that would cause you to come home from Berkeley," Quincy said.

"It's just been really hard on me with both school and my roommate." Sasha took a seat on the living room couch.

"I thought you guys were getting along great." Karen sat in the love seat diagonally across from Sasha, and Quincy sat on the arm of the love seat, next to Karen.

Sasha put her head down and started to cry, while Quincy's head started to spin. He remembered when Sasha had begged him to allow her roommate, Tasha, to stay with her. Quincy had agreed to pay the rent for the two-bedroom apartment so long as Tasha carried her weight around the house. The two got along so well that Sasha left a month before the start of the fall semester just to spend time and hang out with her friend. None of this made sense.

"But even if you guys were arguing, it still docsn't make sense that you would leave in the beginning of the semester and come home," Quincy said.

"Dad, school hasn't gotten off to a good semester. I've been stressed out, and I feel overwhelmed."

"You go to one of the top universities in the country. Of course it's hard. It's supposed to be hard. Pressure either breaks you or it molds you into the person you're meant to be!"

"I know, Dad. I know. It's just that it's hard, and I don't know if I can do it."

"Do what?" Quincy and Karen said in unison.

"This whole college thing. I don't know . . . I don't even know if I want to be a doctor. Part of me thinks that I'm going to school for the wrong reason."

Quincy put his anger in check and looked for the deeper meaning behind his only child's words. He could not focus on how much he had spent so far for Sasha to have a first-class education, only to turn around and throw it back in his face. The Sasha that he and Karen had raised was relentless and goal oriented. She did not shy away from challenges; she advanced. Something was not right, and Quincy needed to figure out what it was. Not even a second later Sasha jumped up unexpectedly.

"I'll be back. I have to use the restroom. You know, long drive," Sasha explained as she walked out of the living room.

"What is going on?" Quincy threw his hands up in protest.

"Let's just hear her out," Karen replied in a calming tone.

"Hear her out? Are you crazy? Our daughter is talking about dropping out of school. There's not too much more of this nonsense that I'm going to listen to."

"You know what your problem is, Q? You're too quick to judge. She's probably being emotional right now. She has a lot on her plate. Just let her talk it out, and she will be back in school before you know it."

"So much for this weekend." Quincy shook his head.

Sasha came back downstairs without the same bounce in her step as before. Quincy also noticed that Sasha had a piece of tissue in her hand, and she wiped her lips.

"Look, I know you guys are worried, but don't be," Sasha said.

"So what were you guys fighting about?" Quincy asked.

"What are you talking about?" Sasha was perplexed.

"What were you and your roommate fighting about?" Karen beat Quincy to the follow-up question.

"Oh, I'm sorry." Sasha contorted her face. "She's just nasty. She doesn't clean up. Her room is a mess, and she's got this foul odor to her."

"I'm not trying to be funny or nothing, but did she all of a sudden forgot how to wash her tail? You've never mentioned this as a problem before. So why move back a month before the start of the semester to be with Stinky?" Quincy said.

"Honey, you guys must be having a different kind of problem," Karen concluded.

"I mean, don't get me wrong. She's a cool person. I just can't deal with it." Sasha shook her head as she stared off into space.

Now Quincy's attention was drawn to Sasha's ensemble. She had on a bright red T-shirt with some gray sweats. Sasha did not even dress like that around the house. There was only one logical explanation for Sasha's erratic behavior. Quincy noticed Karen biting her lip, which meant that she was not buying Sasha's story, either. Quincy knew that many minutes ago Karen had drawn the same conclusion that he had just reached.

"Honey, we're paying a lot of money to send you to one of the best schools in the country. You're too old to be running home just because you don't get along with your roommate," Quincy said.

"She was just being mean to me, and I couldn't handle it. So I decided to come home."

"But that doesn't make any sense. You would come home from Berkeley just because you and your roommate are having problems?" Karen rested Sasha's head on her shoulder. "Sasha, are you pregnant?" Karen just came out and asked. Call it intuition or whatever, but she knew something more was going on.

"Why would you ask me that? I'm telling you that I'm not getting along with my roommate, and you're reading too much into this."

"That's because you didn't come home over your roommate. You came home because either you're pregnant or you're on drugs, and your body language doesn't suggest the latter," Quincy said.

Sasha's face became drenched with tears, which only made the silence more nerve-racking. "Mom, I'm so sorry. I just didn't know what to do."

"How about keeping your legs closed!" Quincy snapped.

"Quincy, don't!" Karen snapped back, cloaked in rage.

But her plea fell on deaf ears. Quincy was not done. "Give me one good reason why I shouldn't hop on a plane right now and kill your little boyfriend for knocking up my daughter?"

Sasha's sobs were uncontrollable. "Because he doesn't know that I'm pregnant!"

# Chapter Five

## *Jamal*

For Jamal, marriage did not come down to man and woman or same sex; marriage involved three components, and the third was God. If God remained at the center of a marriage, then Jamal believed that a couple could weather any storm. Jamal had attended weddings that were literally out of a fairy-tale book. He had attended weddings that were romantic, where the couples were showered with gifts and appliances and enough money to put down on a new home. Jamal had also witnessed those marriages dissolve within a few short years. No one went the distance anymore. His assessment was that couples bowed out before they gave the marriage a chance to flourish. Jamal doubted many people remembered their vows in the tough times. He wondered if he and Chantel would remember their vows.

Jamal and Chantel shared a child together, Jamir, who was three going on thirty. Up until last year, Jamal had thought that Jamir was his biological son. It crushed Jamal to find out that Jamir's true father was Clay, Jamal's late best friend and Chantel's former boyfriend. There was a love that existed between Jamal and Chantel that neither could deny. He loved her, and he loved Jamir and wanted nothing more than to be a family.

Everything had gone well in Jamal and Chantel's relationship until they decided to take Pastor Dawkins's advice and enroll in Pastor Brown's premarital counseling course. What had seemed like a good idea at first turned into a nightmare of biblical proportions.

"All I know is that I don't want some skank texting you," Chantel spewed without eye contact.

This session was supposed to deal with communication, but it was not long before Jamal realized that he and Chantel's communication had disconnected a long time ago.

"We're just friends. I've been knowing Kiesha since grade school," Jamal replied.

"I don't care if you used to play in the sandbox together. I'm going to be your wife, and you should not be texting another woman. It's rude, and it's disrespectful," Chantel yelled in Jamal's ear before she rotated her neck like a snake and sat back in the chair, with folded arms.

The pictures of married couples hung on the walls of Pastor Brown's office like platinum records at record companies. The couples in the pictures served as a testament of Pastor Brown's success. He took great pride in his ability to help couples on the road to marriage to see the many obstacles that stood in their path. Pastor Brown was appointed to the position of premarital counselor by Pastor Dawkins, who at the time felt his unmarried status would hinder more than it would help couples. Pastor Brown understood that so much of marriage was rooted in practicality, and couples like Jamal and Chantel needed both a spiritual and a practical understanding of marriage.

"Let me ask you something." Jamal looked squarely into Pastor Brown's eyes. "Does your wife give her male coworkers rides to work?"

Jamal then looked at Chantel, who sat in silence, with her eyes seemingly fixated on the plethora of plaques on Pastor Brown's wall. "Oh, you ain't got nothing to say, huh?" he noted.

Jamal asked Pastor Brown another question. "Does your wife call her"—Jamal did the quotation marks gesture with his hands—"guy friends baby? Sweetie? And does she—"

"Okay, Jamal, okay! You proved your point. You always got to do extras." Chantel unfolded her arms and threw them up in a tizzy.

"That's because you're always taking me there," Jamal snapped back.

"You know what? Forget this! I ain't marrying your punk-butt. We can cancel this whole thing! I mean, we've already postponed it." Chantel folded her arms again.

"You crazy in your head. My grandparents bought plane tickets from Philly that are nonrefundable. We done paid to have stuffed shells at the reception. We're getting married." Jamal held up one finger. "The only reason why we postponed it was, one, you lost your job, and two, I felt that it was important that we have premarital counseling before we got married. Neither one of us has had great examples of marriage in our lives."

Pastor Brown finally spoke. "You guys have to remember that in marriage there is compromise. To be honest, both of you need to cut down on your single friends when you get married. You guys need to hang out with like-minded couples."

"You hear that, Jamal?" Chantel added.

Jamal bit his bottom lip and resisted the urge to be rude and scornful. In a previous lesson Pastor Brown had warned against saying things out of anger.

"This is one of the most important sessions we'll have." Pastor Brown paused to clear his throat before he continued. "Look at it from this perspective. If you were in a war, what would be the most critical tool used to destroy your enemy?"

"Communication," Chantel said.

"Exactly, because if you can't communicate with your partner, then you can't see where the enemy is coming from and you can't plan for a successful defense. No matter what, you can't break down your lines of communication."

"But, Pastor Brown, I don't think it comes down to communication. This whole thing"—Jamal did a circular motion with his finger—"it comes down to trust."

"I trust you. I just don't trust another woman," Chantel said.

"Then that means you don't trust me, because no matter how fine a woman is, she can't make me cheat on you. I got control of my own actions."

"Ain't nobody saying that you don't have control, but still. Women are trifling, and I know because I used to be one of those girls who didn't care about anything or anyone."

Jamal remembered that season in Chantel's life. It was right after Clay's death. Both Chantel and Jamal took Clay's death hard. With his death, Chantel lost her high school sweetheart and the father of her child. Jamal lost his best friend. Both felt their forbidden love for each other was the root cause of his death. But where Jamal found faith, Chantel found depression, which led to a reckless lifestyle.

"See, this is why I didn't want to do this whole premarital counseling thing," Chantel added, then picked up her purse and fumbled with it. Jamal assumed that she was in search of a tissue.

"Here we go." Jamal leaned back in his chair.

"You right about 'here we go,' because it seems like all we do here is criticize who I am and talk about how I need to change." Chantel caught a tear that had snuck down the side of her cheek.

"No, we don't! We talk about my stuff too," Jamal replied.

"Hold on, Jamal. Let her finish," Pastor Brown interjected. "Go ahead, Chantel."

"I was raised not to expect a man to do anything for me. Now it seems like in order for me to be a good Christian woman, I have to bow down and become a servant."

Jamal didn't just bite his lip; he put his whole hand over his mouth. He had lost count of how many spirited arguments he and Chantel had had over the issue of submission.

Chantel went on. "Whatever! You can say what you want. But it says right there in the Bible, 'Wives, submit to your husbands.' The marriage vows include the word *obey*. That's degrading for a woman to have to say that. Slaves submit, and dogs obey. I ain't doing that, and I definitely ain't saying *obey* at our wedding, either."

"Let's consult the scriptures." Pastor Brown picked up the Bible that was in front of him and started to turn the pages. "Ephesians, chapter five."

Jamal picked up his Bible from his lap and turned to the familiar passage.

"I'll read verse twenty-one, and you guys will take turns reading the rest of the chapter," Pastor Brown said.

Jamal shared his Bible with Chantel. Even though it irked him that Chantel frequently forgot her Bible, Jamal remained silent on the matter.

"Honor Christ by submitting to each other," Pastor Brown said.

Chantel read the next three verses, and then Jamal
came in and finished out the chapter. The scriptures
took on a new light for Jamal, and he hoped that they
would have the same effect on Chantel. When Jamal
finished reading, he and Pastor Brown sat their Bibles
down on Pastor Brown's desk.


"You see, Chantel, the Bible does ask for a wife to
submit to her husband, but it also asks for a husband
to love his wife as Christ loved the church," said Pastor Brown. "God does not want you to submit to a man
who does not honor Christ. God wants you to submit to
a man that has already laid down his life for you, just as
Christ did the church."

Chantel had a hard exterior, but Jamal believed that
Pastor Brown's words found a place in her heart.

"Getting back to today's session, it's important that
you communicate with one another, just like you are
doing now. Communication doesn't always mean that
what you say to each other is pleasant, but it does mean
that you're at least talking out your feelings and frus-
trations. One of the biggest problems I have observed
with marriage is that most couples have forgotten how
to talk to each other," Pastor Brown told them.

Whenever Jamal heard the word *communication*
coupled with the word *marriage,* he always thought
about his mother and father. His father had interpreted
the phrase "forsake all others" loosely, and his mother
had allowed his father to send her to an early grave.

"I think this is a good session," Pastor Brown said.

"Seriously?" Chantel asked.

"Trust me, the couple I worry about is the one that
has problems and never gives voice to them. You guys
should be fine so long as you continue to communi-

cate." Pastor Brown stood up and extended his hand to Jamal. "Well, we'll talk more at our next session."

"Thank you, Pastor Brown." Jamal shook his hand, in amazement at the wisdom and practicality Pastor Brown possessed. Pastor Brown had about the same build as Jamal, but he was a little older and wore some thick bifocals. Yet Jamal revered him.

"Thank you." Chantel extended her hand and retrieved it before Pastor Brown had gotten a firm grasp of it.

She stormed out Pastor Brown's office, as if she was trying to make it to the bank before it closed. She pushed through the double doors and made her way under the archway and down the front steps of the cathedral.

"You forgot that we took my car?" Jamal called as he jogged down the steps after Chantel.

"I haven't forgotten anything. I remember being independent and having my own place and my own income. Now it seems like I'm going backwards." Chantel did not break her stride in her rant.

"Hold up." Jamal finally caught up to Chantel and took her by the arm. "Where's this coming from?"

"This is exactly why I have problems with church. You expect me to give up my independence and become submissive and less than your equal."

"Have I ever asked that from you?"

"No, but you're real clever. I wanted a September wedding, my dream wedding, and you said no, that you wanted to do premarital counseling. Now I see why you got me in premarital counseling. So you can indoctrinate me and have me at home, cooking, cleaning, and baking cookies."

"Heck, naw. You can't bake cookies nohow," Jamal said as he let out a giggle.

Chantel punched Jamal in the arm. "I'm not playing with you. I don't want to become some subservient woman with no say-so. This ain't the fifties."

"I'm marrying you for who you are. I'm not asking you to be nothing other than yourself. I just want to do the right thing."

"Oh really? Is that why we're living together? Because last time I checked, the church frowned upon that," Chantel said.

"You know I only did that to help you out after you lost your job."

"I also know that those late-night creeps into my room are not for nothing."

Chantel's words punctured Jamal's spirit, and self-righteousness was left in its wake. As much as Jamal tried to rationalize why he had decided to let Chantel move in with him,there was no escaping the fact that the decision was not one that God would be proud of. Jamal wondered how he and Chantel would build a marriage if were not living right and they couldn't communicate.

# Chapter Six

## *Will*

*One Week until the Men's Retreat . . .*

"Don't come back over here, cuz." A firm threat from a member of Will's former gang.

Will considered the severity of the threat as the Oster two-speed clippers cruised at a low altitude and trimmed off the corkscrews of hair that gathered on the crown of his client's head. The Oster was followed by a hairbrush to smooth out the surface. As the hair descended to the floor, Will put down the brush, and with his free hand, he grabbed a mini-brush to dust off the excess hair from his client's shoulders. The line at the barber college steadily grew. Will focused on the client in the chair and continued to prune the hair in an effort to create an even low-cut hairstyle.

Will's mind was divided into three compartments: his client's haircut, the risk Will took to see his family, and what God expected from him. Not that long ago Will could remember a time when he didn't fear death, because there was nothing worth living for. Will still had little concern about death, but every day hope grew inside of him. He wondered if his life would be struck down before he even got a chance to enjoy the freedom and peace he had found in Christ.

Will thought about the number fifteen hundred. Fifteen hundred represented the amount of hours Will needed to complete in order to become a licensed barber. Every customer brought him closer to full-time work as a barber. He appreciated Quincy, who bankrolled his tuition and living situation.

For the first time in his life, someone believed in Will and demonstrated it through actions. The idea of being independent of the hustle game and independent from the family business motivated Will to both study hard and work hard.

Will attributed his barber skills to his meticulous nature and his desire to work in the spirit of excellence. He stayed focused on the ebb and flow of patrons who came into the shop for a cheap haircut. Most of the chatter that went on in the barbershop was fruitless. Will had no interest in the social side of the barber profession.

Will was finishing up the haircut when Joshua walked in the door with a backpack on his shoulders and a skateboard under his arm. Russell, the director of the barber school, was empathic about Will's situation and allowed Joshua to come to the shop from school every day while Will worked.

"What up, man?" Will gave his brother a handshake that ended with the snap of their fingers. "Go ahead and go back there and get started." Will pointed to the break room in the shop. Joshua followed his older brother's orders without hesitation.

"Thanks, man, and good luck with getting your license," Will's customer said as he got up and examined his haircut in the mirror Will had positioned behind him.

"Thank you. I appreciate that." Will shook the man's hand, and then he shook out the excess hair on the barber's cape before he made his way to the back of the shop. Will discovered that Joshua had already taken a seat at the empty table in the back of the room.

Joshua opened his backpack and removed his math textbook. With his foot on the skateboard, he began to complete his problems. Adjacent to Joshua was the shop's refrigerator. Will opened the refrigerator door and took out a turkey on wheat sandwich and a bottle of vitamin water.

"Here. Eat up." Will handed Joshua the sandwich and water and took a seat at the table.

Joshua wasted no time; he unwrapped the sandwich and took a monstrous bite. Will smiled as he observed his brother with contentment. It felt good to be able to provide his brother with some semblance of stability.

"How's everything at home?" Will asked.

"Mom and Dad are fighting again," Joshua said in between bites.

That was not an earth-shattering revelation. The eye of the storm dwelled on Atlantic Avenue, to the point where whenever Will's parents acted normal, he would think that they had been invaded by an alien life form.

"How's my baby sis?" Will asked.

"She cries every time they argue, and her screams could break glass."

Will loved his baby sister, Elisha. She favored his mother. While Will had known only the addict version of his mother, his baby sister looked like an innocent version of Carroll. Elisha enabled Will to consider what his mother's life was like before she turned to drugs. Elisha also reminded Will of how shallow his relationship was with his mother. He had never asked Carroll about her dreams or aspirations.

As much as Will loved his sister, he doubted that he could raise a baby girl on his own. It was not hard for him to be with Joshua. Will just did the opposite of whatever he had seen his father do. Girls were more complex to Will, and in truth he had not met a girl he could be in a serious relationship with, let alone raise.

"I'm hoping that Dad will let you come live with me," Will told his brother.

Joshua put his head down, as if the world he lived in was without hope.

"I wish you were there, bro. We could be a family again," Joshua said.

"Listen, Josh, I know your intentions are good, but that's a fantasy. Too much has happened, and I've seen too much to believe that things can change."

"I thought you were supposed to believe anything is possible?" Josh asked.

"I believe in wisdom, and the Bible talks about being wise, and when you have people who can't own up to their own mistakes, then there is no hope."

"You don't give up on your family," Joshua replied.

"We ain't never been a family, Josh. I don't know what we are, but it sure ain't no family." Will put his head down to fight back his anger.

"Dad's home now," Joshua replied.

"We'll see for how long."

"I think it's for good, and you know our father. He won't say it, but he misses you, and maybe we can work things out if we all lived together."

"Look, Josh, I know you want us to be a family, but you got to understand something. I'm trying to turn my life around, and I can't do that if I'm living at home. I can't. I'm sorry." Will tried to hold back his irritation.

"All you care about is yourself. You got a place some rich dude is paying for, and you can care less." Joshua started to rock back and forth, with his fist clenched. Will knew his brother was holding back both his tears and his fists.

The words had come out of Joshua's mouth, and it was Joshua's voice that had said them, but those were someone else's thoughts and feelings. Joshua was all twisted inside, and Will did not know how to help.

"Most of my friends wish they had their father in their lives, even if he had been in and out of prison like our dad. Don't the Bible teach forgiveness? When are you going to forgive our father?"

That was a good question, one that Will did not have the answer to. He harbored a lot of hatred toward his father, and the more he thought about it, the more he realized he even harbored hatred toward his mother too.

"Just because our father is somewhat in our lives doesn't mean that's a good thing. What example has he set for us? Is there anything that he has taught us that doesn't involve getting over on people?"

"He taught us how to survive, and you know we wouldn't have if he didn't."

"See, that's the thing. That's not enough for me. I don't just want to survive. I want to thrive, and the life our father offers is no real life at all."

Will felt like he was talking to a younger version of himself. He leaned back in his chair and watched Joshua eat.

"You know that D-Loc got shot," Joshua said.

"I heard, but what's that got to do with you?"

"Nothing. I'm just saying. He was a friend of the family and he—"

"He was never a friend of the family. He was a parasite, and you can't expect to have a happy ending when all you've done is brought destruction."

"He looked out for us, though."

"He used us, and you can't tell me that life is better with him around than without him." Will bent down to adjust his shoes for comfort. He saw a blue shoestring hanging out of Joshua's backpack. Will looked at Joshua's pure white shoes. "What's this?"

Will removed the shoestring from Joshua's backpack. He did not wait for Joshua to respond. He beat Joshua to the punch and snatched the backpack from his younger brother before Joshua even had a chance. When Will opened the backpack, he found a royal blue T-shirt and a royal blue bandanna. He laid the items on the table before he removed a green folder with the word *Untouchables* written across it.

Will swung at his brother with the intent to smack him on the back of the head. It was only in a split second of self-control that Will grabbed Joshua by his head instead and pulled him close, within inches of his nose. "Have you lost your mind?"

Joshua responded to Will's question only with deep breaths. Joshua could not shake free from Will's grip.

"Are you trying to throw your life away?"

"Man, get off me! Let my shirt go." Joshua tried to fight his way out of Will's grip.

Will released his grip to avoid drawing the attention of the people in the shop. Joshua adjusted his shirt. "You don't realize what you've done. You've just handed your life over to the devil."

"What am I supposed to do? You know I can't just live there and not be down."

"So you want to be down? Is that what you're telling me?"

"I ain't had no choice, bro. I had to. Everybody on the set says that you betrayed your family when you went into the church."

"I couldn't care less what they say. They didn't make me, and they don't control my destiny, either. Don't make the same mistakes I made. You're better than that. You have a choice. You just can't see that."

Will started to become physically ill from what he'd heard. His brother talked about the set as if he had been in it for years and as if the Untouchables were really a family. His concept of family was so distorted.

"Don't you want more out of your life?" Will asked.

"Wanting and having are two different things. I just don't want to be afraid. I want to walk the streets and get respect. I can't get that being some poor boy in the hood."

"The devil is the master of deception. He had me thinking that stealing was the only way that I would have anything of value. He had me thinking that being in a gang was the only way I would ever be anything of value. It was a lie, Josh. It's all a lie. I'm more of a man now than I've ever been because of Christ."

Joshua did not say a word. He just put his head down.

"What are you going to do if they ask you to kill someone? Can you live with yourself?"

Joshua did not reply. He just kept his head down.

"D-Loc was one of the most feared men on the streets, and he's dead before he reached thirty. Thirty, Josh." Will put his hand on Joshua's shoulder and eased him up so that he could look at his brother eye to eye. "You want to live to see thirty?"

Joshua shrugged his shoulders. "Not if it's going to be the same old stuff. I just want to be like you."

"What's wrong with being like me now?"

"Man, it's not realistic. I ain't going to meet some rich guy to bless me with a new situation."

"You don't know what God has in store for you. Does Dad know about you being in a gang?"

"Yeah."

"And what does he say?"

"He doesn't agree with it, but he says I got to do what I got to do."

Will leaned back in his chair and shook his head in disbelief. A line had formed at the barber college again. Will had to go back to work. "We ain't finished with this. Josh, you got a chance to do something with your life. And if it takes my last breath, then I'm going to make sure that you do."

The sound of an aggressive horn broke up Will's cathartic moment with his brother. He looked outside and spotted his father in a new Cadillac coupe. There was only one way he could explain having it. Joshua ran out of the barbershop like a kid who had heard the bell sound on the last day of school. With purposeful strides, Will followed right behind, shaking his head. His father let down the window to put out the ashes of his Dutch and then took another puff with a smile, as if he had just gotten away with murder.

The image reminded Will of all those years that he had stolen cars and had never got caught, while his father had always seemed to get caught. It was because Will was smarter. His father knew more about cars than most manuals. It was because Will always had a goal, and he never deviated from that goal. His goal was to steal a car and get it off the streets as soon as humanly possible, get paid, and disappear. His father, on the other hand, wanted to live a lifestyle that he had never had and would never have.

"Hey, boy, what do you say we go and get a couple of those burritos at King Taco?" Will's father said to Joshua.

That was all it took for Joshua to make his way to the passenger side of the vehicle without hesitation.

"Joshua, come here, man," Will said.

"Man, don't get involved," Odell replied.

Will addressed his father with his hands and not his eyes. "Man, I don't got nothing to say to you except that

I'll pray for you, because you got some real issues pulling a gun on your own son."

"Son or not, I won't take being disrespected. And you ain't so perfect yourself."

"I know, which is why I stay praying, and I pray for you because in the end we all going to have to give account for God, and you have systemically destroyed this family in more ways than one."

Joshua stopped and stood frozen in his tracks, not sure what to do in this situation. Will's father, on the other hand, put the car in park and got out. He stopped within striking distance and allowed Will to consider the head and shoulder size advantage Odell had over him, but Will did not back down, nor was he intimidated.

"It seems like I'm going to have to show you who the alpha dog is in this family," Odell growled.

"A year ago you came to this shop and told me that you were a changed man. You remember that? What happened?"

"Will, you got me?" a customer yelled from inside the barbershop.

"In a minute. Just wait in the chair," Will said.

"The false sense of freedom wore off. The truth is that I'm not truly free, even out here, and people won't let me change, so what else is there? I had to wake up," Odell said. And with that statement, Will's father backed up, as if he was scared to turn his back on his son. "Get in the car now, Josh."

Josh got in the car, and the emotional tug-of-war was over. Will stood in the parking lot even after his father sped off, leaving burning tire track marks in his wake. He was transfixed by what had transpired. Will wanted so much for his father to go back to prison, where he could destroy his own life and not the lives of those around him.

Will walked back into the shop with his head spinning from the revelation. His brother was in a gang. The only question was, what would Will have to do to get his brother out?

# Chapter Seven

## *Quincy*

The store smelled like old shoe polish and looked like it hadn't been dusted in quite a while. Within the confines of the gun shop was every tool built for destruction, and Quincy got giddy at the sight of it. Quincy held the Taurus 24-pistol firmly in his hand. The power to control someone's fate lay in his hands, and Quincy felt like a god, small *g*.

"Don't you think that the 'disapproving father with the gun' act is a little cliché?" Jamal asked while positioned next to the sporting wear.

"I admit that it's not the most novel idea I've come up with, but it will work, nonetheless." Quincy aimed the gun toward a mannequin that was dressed in army fatigues.

"Brother Page, I don't think that you have consulted the Lord on this matter. I know that the enemy is at work," Chauncey said.

"I already know what God will say. He'll tell me to turn the other cheek or something like that. . . . He knows my heart." Quincy then looked at Will. "What about this one?"

"Jamming problems," Will said.

Quincy put down the Glock pistol and picked up the Beretta that the gun dealer had sat on top of the display case for Quincy's viewing. "Now we're talking. This is some Mel Gibson *Lethal Weapon* type of madness."

"Beretta nine millimeter has both double and single action. Firm grip and can hold fifteen rounds. Its design came from military. . . ." Will stopped when he looked at Jamal.

Jamal made a hand gesture to Will to not encourage Quincy. Jamal walked over to a knife rack and started to examine the different knives. "I know this might be difficult, but Sasha is what? Twenty? She's a grown woman."

"She's too young to throw her life away. She was being irresponsible and reckless," Quincy said.

"Where I'm from, we call that being something else," Will said.

"The Bible has also got a word for it," Chauncey said before Quincy shot him a disconcerted look.

Quincy could not understand where he had gone wrong. Private schools, piano lessons, study groups, and church activities. He and Karen had raised their daughter not to be passive, not to live in a constant state of waiting. Waiting for her check to arrive, waiting for her EBT card, waiting for her Section 8 housing to get approved. Waiting for her Prince Charming, who was a cross between 50 Cent and Obama with an obese bank account. He had raised Sasha not to be a recipient in life, but a participant.

"Look, I know that the Bible teaches that we're to respect life and that abortion is wrong, but honestly, I wouldn't be mad if she decided to have an abortion." Quincy sat the handgun on the table and hit the counter. "This is my baby girl! She can play Beethoven just by the sense of sound. We go to a Mexican restaurant, and she can order off the menu with fluent Spanish. She can even break down the fine points of the health care debate. I don't want this for her."

"It doesn't mean that her life is over," Jamal said.

"It means that *my* life is over. I just got used to walking around in my drawers. My wife and I christened every room in our house."

"That's so good that you christened the house. God will bless you two," Chauncey said, aloof.

"Who invited him?" Quincy looked at Jamal and Will, who in response shrugged their shoulders. "I'm not ready to be a grandfather. I'm still trying to get my grown and sexy on. I don't need another reminder that I'm getting old."

"I'm sorry, Q, but it just seems like this is more about you and less about Sasha," Jamal said.

"Look, you try raising your child and giving them every advantage they need to be successful in life, only for them to throw that back in your face by getting pregnant their sophomore year in college. It's easy to coach from the cheap seats. Talk to me when you're on the field. Until then, step!" Quincy made a hand gesture for Jamal to step off.

"Look, Q, there's no need to get defensive. We're just trying to help," Jamal replied.

"Yeah, we got you're back, Grandpa Q," Will teased.

That marked the first time someone had muttered the statement that Quincy was old. That he would never play four downs in the Super Bowl was a bitter pill to swallow. Being old meant that Quincy would never have to learn the triangle offense, and he was too old to audition for *American Idol*. He thought of the loss of those days, and then of the days that lay ahead, the discount breakfasts and the more frequent checkups. Quincy ebbed and flowed from contentment to contempt.

"Look, we all make mistakes, but God can fix any situation to the point where it would seem like that was His plan all along. Just give them a chance," Chauncey said.

"When is the guy coming over?" Will asked.

"Saturday." Quincy hit his head and then scratched it. "I guess I should be thankful that there is only one father, instead of two potential fathers, like on those television shows. When she was in school, I used to tell her that no man was going to buy a pair of worn shoes. She made it through high school on that analogy. I hoped that she would be able to survive college on that same logic."

"Q, that doesn't mean that you did something wrong as a parent. It just means that she made a poor decision as an adult," Jamal said.

Another sign that Quincy had gotten old. He held up the gun to the surfer-looking employee with a Mohawk. "I'll take this one," Quincy said.

"Okay, sir. Well, we have a ten-day waiting period. I'll just need your driver's license and a thumbprint, and you have to take a HSC test," the employee said.

"A test? What is this? The DMV?" Quincy placed the gun on the counter, reached into his pocket, removed seven one-hundred-dollar bills, and placed them on the counter.

"I'm sorry, sir. We have a ten-day waiting period," the employee repeated.

Quincy reached into his pocket and pulled out another hundred-dollar bill.

"We have a ten-day waiting period," the employee said again with a smile.

"I ain't trying to be funny or nothing, but since when did the gun store grow a conscience? Doc, you got enough guns to supply the Afghan army. You probably have some missing WMDs in here."

"California has a very strict gun policy, and you have to demonstrate an understanding of the safety procedures before I can let you own one," the employee informed him.

"Oh no, I'm not planning to use it. I just want to scare this boy. You know the enraged father routine. You know? You don't even have to give me bullets."

"Look, dude, unless you're going to take the test and wait the ten days, I can't do nothing for you," the employee said as he opened the display case, prepared to put the guns back where he had gotten them from.

"Hold on," Jamal said to the employee before he turned to Quincy. "I know you're not about to go this route. If you think it's bad being a father, imagine being a grandfather. Then imagine being a grandfather in San Quentin."

"He's got a point, Q," Will said.

"Amen! Finally, somebody talking with some sense," Chauncey said.

Will, Jamal, and Quincy all looked at Chauncey, as if to tell him to shut up. Jamal's statement gave Quincy pause. This was not a Madea film. This was real life, and he could not shoot his way out of the problem. Of course, there might be another alternative. Quincy looked at the employee. "You wouldn't happen to have a rocket launcher, would you?" he asked.

# Chapter Eight

## *Titus*

After the eight o'clock service, Titus greeted his members in front of the pulpit. Titus did this every week, though he was exhausted after his sermons, just to let the people know that he had not lost his common touch. Even though his schedule was full with speaking engagements, which usually meant he had to hop on a flight immediately after the service, Titus still took a few minutes after each service to shake hands with those in his congregation who were not in a rush to go home or go to brunch. Grace accompanied Titus. She stepped into her role of first lady nicely. She was kind and pleasant, but above all, she was genuine.

Mother Ruth remained a loyal supporter of Greater Anointing. At eighty-three, she made sure not to miss a service. Mother Ruth approached Titus and made a gesture with her lips, and the six-foot-five-inch frame of Titus bent down for her to kiss him on the cheek. Aside from Jesus, only a strong woman of faith could cause a man of Titus's stature to stoop down.

"God bless you, Mother Ruth. How are things?" Titus said after he stood back up straight.

"I'm fine. The doctor says my cholesterol is in good shape."

"All right now. Now, don't go off to no Roscoe's or R & J's Soul Food," Titus said after he let out a snicker.

"I won't, Pastor. I won't." Ruth made her way out the side exit.

Titus glanced at Grace. She had a disposition as gloomy as an overcast day, cloaked in a Christian smile. Sister Norworthy had just walked by Grace to get to him without saying so much as a word.

"God bless you, Sister Norworthy." Titus shook her hand with both hands. "Doesn't the first lady look great?" Titus pointed back to his wife so that Sister Norworthy would acknowledge her.

"Oh. I'm sorry, First Lady. I didn't see you. Those shoes are cute." Sister Norworthy pointed toward the suede wraparound Jimmy Choos that Titus had just bought Grace.

"Thank you, and you look great, Sister Norworthy." Grace said.

Sister Norworthy turned her attention back to Titus. "Pastor, I was wondering, when are you going to start preaching the evening service again?" Sister Norworthy was referring to the seven o'clock service on Sunday evening. Titus used to preach all three services on Sunday, but since he'd married Grace, Titus had preached only the eight o'clock and the eleven o'clock services. He allowed other ministers to preach the seven o'clock. Sometimes Titus would allow visiting ministers to preach the eight o'clock as well.

"I don't know, Sister Norworthy. Maybe someday soon." Titus flashed a halfhearted smile.

Sister Norworthy walked away with displeasure written clearly across her face.

"God bless you, Pastor Dawkins," Tamika Cain said as she stood and blocked Titus's view of Grace.

"Excuse me one second, Sister Cain." Titus took Grace by the hand and pulled her into Tamika's view.

"Oh, I am so sorry, First Lady. I didn't see you," Tamika said.

"That's quite all right!" Grace said.

This was a blatant act of disrespect, which Titus did not tolerate toward his wife. Grace remained gracious, as her name implied, as that was her nature.

"When are you going to teach Bible study again?" Tamika asked.

"Not for another month, Sister Cain. I have to go out of town on Monday and speak at a convocation." Titus put his arm around Grace. "It's going to be hard, though, leaving this beautiful woman at home."

Titus's gesture was greeted with rolled eyes from Tamika.

"I'm sure she'll be fine," Tamika said.

"God bless you," Grace said with a smile that conveyed the opposite of what she truly wanted to say.

A lot of the women of the congregation shared similar sentiments with Sister Norworthy and Tamika. The congregation took Titus's engagement to Grace like a bitter pill swallowed with honey. A lot of members uprooted themselves and left, and Pastor Dawkins wondered if Sister Norworthy's and Tamika's lack of respect for the first lady was only the beginning of much larger issues.


Later on that night, at an hour when no one called unless it was an emergency, the phone rang. The phone woke Titus and Grace out of their sleep in a panic.

"Hello?" Grace asked, half asleep.

Deep breaths.

"Hello? Who is this?"

Deep breaths.

"I'm hanging up!"

The unknown caller beat Grace to the hanging up, and two minutes later the phone rang again.

"You're going to have to get that under control, Titus," Grace said, with her back turned toward Titus.

Titus wanted to play coy, but his wife was too smart, and an insult to her intelligence would have added unnecessary tension. Titus remembered when the phone rang at all hours of the night at his parents' house. The callers were desperate women who wanted to be soothed and comforted by their pastor. Titus ignored the phone calls, while his father didn't.

# Chapter Nine

## Chauncey

Chauncey did not care to miss a Saturday night shut-in prayer service, especially a week before the Men's Retreat. The six-to-midnight prayer session that followed the men's prayer breakfast made for a powerful evening. It would set the tone for the week that lay ahead, to the point where he even contemplated whether or not he should go through with his date. Of course, Gabrielle, a woman he'd met on Soulmates.com, seemed to be too nice of a woman to defer their rendezvous. He reveled in the fact that the future Mrs. McClendon could be on her way.

Chauncey sat in his champagne Cadillac and drummed up a beat on his steering wheel while in the parking lot of John's Incredible Pizza. He had been to Buena Park on many occasions as a result of church picnics at Knott's Berry Farm, but he had never been to this pizza spot, which seemed childlike. He took Gabrielle's word that this was the perfect meeting place.

*Lord, I pray that nothing is wrong with this woman. Though she may look a little young, I pray that she is of legal age. I also pray that she doesn't have any addictions or mental instabilities and that she has always been a woman. In Jesus's name, amen.*

Chauncey concluded his prayer, and a gray minivan with a dented front bumper pulled up. It was clear that the minivan had not been to a car wash in quite some time. The passenger side door slid open, and juice boxes and empty water bottles fell out. A boy who looked no more than three years old jumped out of the minivan and landed on the juice boxes. He was followed by a little girl who was not much older than him, with hair as wild as Patti LaBelle's in 1983. Then there was a teenage girl with long braids who got out of the front passenger seat. Chauncey felt a twinge in his stomach at the sight of her and the possible connection.

*Lord, Jesus, give me strength. Please let these kids belong to someone else.*

Of course, God, who, Chauncey was convinced, had a sense of humor, did not honor his request. Gabrielle, his date, emerged from the driver's side of the minivan and walked to the passenger side and picked up the little boy, holding him in her arms. He recognized her from the pictures.

Chauncey turned on his engine with the intent of driving off before he was spotted, but when he looked into the rearview, Gabrielle waved at him.

*Dagnabbit, I've been made.*

Normally, Chauncey did not endorse lying, but in the time that it took Gabrielle to travel over to his car with her children, he thought of three possible lies. He had started applying meat to the bone of one of them when Gabrielle arrived at his driver's side window.

"Thank you so much for coming," Gabrielle said through the window.

Her smile convicted Chauncey. The least he could do was carry out his original plan. Chauncey got out of the car and put on the fakest smile possible. "God bless you." He gestured toward Gabrielle like he was about to hug her, but he could not maneuvered around her with the baby in her arms.

"Say hello, Troy," Gabrielle said to the young boy she held in her arms. She then started to wave Troy's hand for him.

"God bless you, little man." Chauncey stuck his hand out for a high five, but Troy instead grabbed Chauncey's bottom lip.

"Don't do that." Gabrielle smacked Troy's hand away.

"Oh, that's okay," Chauncey said with a chuckle.

"Well, you ready?" Gabrielle asked.

Chauncey tried to think of the various lies he had conjured up. But all he had was gibberish. "Yeah, sure," he replied.

"Okay, well, let's hurry." Gabrielle started to walk toward the entrance.

He just had to survive a meal. Across the street was Knott's Berry Farm theme park. Chauncey likened his current dating experience to riding a roller coaster. Just when he felt like he had reached the peak, the next thing he knew, he was being plunged into the deep abyss of a flawed Internet dating system, where people could lie about their age and status.

As he entered the picturesque John's Incredible Pizza, Chauncey's nightmare only grew more horrific. Inside the room where children had an opportunity to make their own pizza was a banner that read HAPPY BIRTHDAY, TROY.

Not only had Gabrielle lied about her village of children, but she had also lied about their meeting being a date. His humiliation peaked when Troy, who still had not said anything to him, came and brought him a birthday hat to put on.

"Aww, how cute," said some girl who Chauncey did not know.

"Well, I don't know if that would fit on me all that well." Chauncey examined the cone-shaped hat with the elastic string, as well as his two-piece hunter green suit, but Troy was persistent, and he even tried to put the hat on Chauncey's head.

"Okay, okay, I'll wear it." Chauncey then proceeded to put the hat on top of his head.

With a birthday hat on and an uncooked pizza in front of him that needed to be assembled, Chauncey wondered if there was a bottom to all of this. While Chauncey tried to figure it all out, Troy climbed on top of him and sat on his lap.

"Are you the father?" a strange man asked.

"Heck, no. I'm not the father." Chauncey repented to himself for the near expletive.

The man started to chuckle. "Aren't you the lucky one!"

"Why do you ask?" Chauncey questioned.

"Tatiyana and Kaiya are my daughters." He pointed to the two girls. "My name is Chris." Chris gave Chauncey an awkward handshake that contorted his fingers in all sorts of ways.

"How many kids does she have?" Chauncey asked.

"She got five kids. She got a set of twins who live with their grandparents in North Carolina," Chris replied.

Five kids without a ring. Chauncey could not fathom what would possess her to have so much unprotected sex. How could any woman in this day and age expect to be successful with five kids and no husband?

"I had to do some investigating on some *Law & Order* type of stuff to get to the truth," Chris offered.

"Why did you stay with her?"

"Because she is fine, and she was getting those county checks and child support checks from the other baby daddy. I had it made while I was out of work, but not too long after Kaiya was born, I bounced. Gabbie was too much drama for me."

Chauncey no longer saw the man in front of him as a man, but as a statistic. "How often do you visit your kids?"

"Often. At first I didn't, but then I became a changed man."

"What happened? Did you find the Lord?"

"Naw, child support. They tried to take a brotha's driver's license and everything. There's only so many times you can quit a job to avoid paying child support before your family stops loaning you money." The guy patted Chauncey on the back. "Take my advice. If you don't want to pay, put a helmet on your soldier."

It took Chauncey a minute to realize what helmet and what soldier Chris was speaking of. He did not know that such a brute was capable of a figurative analogy.

Gabrielle walked up with drinks in her hands. "Don't be trying to scare him off, Chris." Gabrielle sat a drink down in front of Chauncey.

Chauncey stood up and handed Troy over to Chris, then made his way toward Gabrielle. "I need to talk to you."

"You want to play me in air hockey? It's impossible to score on me," Gabrielle said.

*With five kids, evidently not.* With his hand on her back, Chauncey led Gabrielle outside the pizza-making room and into the video game area.

"Listen, I'm sorry, but this isn't going to work," Chauncey said.

"Chris is such a hater. I swear!" Gabrielle rolled her eyes.

"You have a lot of kids, who you did not tell me about." Chauncey struggled to get his words out in fear of offending the young single mother.

"Chauncey, you seem like a nice dude, but if you can't handle that I got three kids—"

"Five!" Chauncey put his hands on top of his head in disbelief.

"What a hater, dude." Gabrielle turned around and mouthed something to Chris, who only smiled and waved back at her.

Chauncey used this time to flee, taking off in a brisk walk toward the exit.

"Chauncey! Chauncey!" Gabrielle shouted, but Chauncey did not break his stride.

He was through with online dating, and he was through with his search for a wife. At least for now.

# Chapter Ten

## *Quincy*

*Two Days until the Retreat . . .*

"I can't take this, Lord," Quincy said, as if the Lord were sitting in the chair across from his desk. He lifted up his desk calendar, which was covered with scribbled-in meetings and deadlines. He removed a copper key from underneath his desk. He then proceeded to unlock the bottom drawer, and a bottle of 150-proof vodka rolled. It was more of a gut check. Could Quincy face down his temptation another day and not give in?

"Two hundred eleven days," Quincy said to himself. He had no patience to work twelve steps; he had just made up his mind to rid himself of anything toxic. Quincy did not classify himself as an alcoholic. He had moments of weakness and moments when the pressure of a multimillion-dollar contract got to him. In those moments Quincy found solace in the bottle. For the last 211 days, Quincy had found strength in God and in a support system that included Karen and his three brothers of the Gospels. Quincy had seen the results that his faith could produce. He had ridden out the recession virtually unscathed, and to God be the glory.

Quincy had come to the realization that Karen would never be able to understand why he was so embattled and so bitter. It was not a simple case of a disappointed father whose daughter had gotten pregnant and thus had put her plans for world conquest on permanent hold. It was more of a revelation that Quincy had fallen victim to the playboy theory. The theory was that if a guy was a player, then when he became a father, he would automatically have a daughter. That way he would be condemned to spend the rest of his life fending off cold-blooded players like himself who had their eyes on his daughter.

There was a knocked at the door. Quincy knew it was his daughter because she always gave three quick knocks on the door.

"Enter!" Quincy said.

Sasha opened the door with a solemn look on her face. "Daddy, I know you're disappointed." Sasha took a seat on Quincy's lap like she was a little girl.

"You need to expand your vocabulary. I was disappointed when you quit the varsity basketball team. I was disappointed when you forgot my birthday. Honey, I'm furious!"

"I made a mistake. You and Mom have made mistakes as well," Sasha said.

"Your mother and I have made some mistakes, but we are adults, and so are you. Just because we were going through things does not give you the right to get pregnant," Quincy snapped.

"It was stupid, Dad. I get it. But didn't you do stupid things in college that you later regretted?"

Quincy thought about the time when he and his friends used to randomly steal the Bob's Big Boy statue and place it on people's front lawns. He thought back to the time he took a job as a door-to-door knives salesman, which lasted all of two days. He thought about those things before he responded to Sasha.

"Yes, I've done some stupid things, but none of them were life altering, like what you have done."

Sasha's only response was a shamefully bowed head and a slump of the shoulders. Quincy could not let her off that easy. She had to understand the repercussions of her actions. She needed to know what she had lost and what still could be gained.

"I mean, I'm not trying to be funny or nothing, but didn't you and your mother have a talk about your womanhood and how precious it is?"

"She did have the talk with me, but I think it would've been better if you'd done it."

"I don't know about that. All I would've said is, 'Don't march your soldier into battle without a helmet.'" Quincy shrugged his shoulders.

"Daddy, I need you by my side. I don't know if I can do this without you and Mom."

"What you need is the Lord. I'm by your side, princess. Your mother and I both are, but I've seen God do some amazing things. I've seen Him turn the most undesired situation into a blessing."

A knock on the door interrupted their father-daughter moment. It was Karen. She always knocked on the door like a woodpecker before entering. She must've figured that the several knocks gave someone ample enough time to brace themselves for her entry.

"Sasha, there's some guy downstairs that's here to see you," Karen said.

"A *guy* downstairs?" Quincy's stomach turned into another knot. "What guy?" Quincy's head made a sharp turn, and he stared at Sasha.

"My boyfriend, Dwight. I flew him down here to meet you guys," Sasha explained.

Quincy wished that his daughter's boyfriend was front page news. .

"Sasha, what's wrong with you? Why on earth would you think that it's okay to fly your boyfriend down here? We're still adjusting to the news that you're pregnant!" Out of disappointment, Quincy moved Sasha off of his knee.

"Dad, we're going to be a family. I talked to him about it, and he wants to be a father."

Anyone who had known Sasha longer than five seconds knew that she came from wealth. Most men would've headed for the hills in Dwight's situation. Quincy vowed to find out what the ulterior motive was behind Dwight's visit and his willingness to become Sasha's baby daddy.

"Sasha, honey, it's rude to keep your guest waiting. Your father and I will be down in a minute," Karen said. As soon as Sasha left the room, Karen closed the door behind her so that she and Quincy could have some privacy. "You can't hide in here all day. You got to come out and face this," she said.

"Boyfriend? Another secret she kept from her parents. So much for openness. I can't understand it. We've always raised her to take responsibility for her actions."

"At least she knows who the father is and we don't have to go on *Maury*." Karen tried to fix her earrings. "Look, we both have done stupid things, and what Sasha did was just as stupid, but we can't be divided now. We need to pull together as a family."

The issue between Quincy and Karen regarding their affairs was still very sore. They had spent this past year trying to believe that what happened was an isolated incident. What happened was a moment of weakness and a desperate plea for salvation for a marriage that had become cold.

"Come on, babe. I need you to make it through." Karen took Quincy by the hand, and he willing left his office.

As they walked down the winding staircase, Quincy got a good look at the possible father, and he took a deep sigh. Unless Sasha was about to kiss him and turn him into a prince, Quincy was staring at a broken version of Lil Wayne.

"Daddy, this is Dwight."

"Pleasure to meet you." Quincy said the lie effortlessly.

"Yeah, Sasha has told me a lot about you. She told me that you're a go-get-it type of dude. A true hustler." Dwight tried to give Quincy an urban handshake, which only entangled his fingers. Dwight then released Quincy's fingers and stood with his arm around Sasha's shoulders.

Quincy shook his head. "I'm a businessman. I build things, while hustlers take shortcuts. I don't equate the hard work that I do to that of a hustler. It's just hard work." Quincy could tell that his comments rocked Dwight like a body shot from George Foreman. "Well, we got a reservation for three." Quincy looked at Sasha. "Sasha, honey, let's go."

"Where y'all eating at?" Dwight said.

"We are having dinner at the Four Seasons. There's a Popeye's about five miles from here."


At dinner it was clear that Dwight was a fish out of water. The only reason he did not violate the restaurant's strict dress code was that Quincy made him pull his pants up and put on a collared shirt and a sports coat before they left the house.

Even the meal was something that Dwight was not used to, and he took only a few bites of his baked chicken before he flagged down the waiter. "Hey, do you got any Rooster?"

The Asian waitress looked at Dwight quizzically. "Rooster?"

"Yeah, Red Rooster Louisiana Hot Sauce." Dwight did a poor hand gesture to convey what a hot sauce bottle looked at like. "Never mind," Dwight mumbled, abandoning his request after the Asian woman shrugged her shoulders.

"So, Dwight, how did you and Sasha meet?" Karen asked.

"At a Sigma party," Dwight replied.

"You're a Sigma?" Quincy asked.

"No. I'm a DJ, so I do all their functions."

"So you don't even go to Berkeley?" Karen asked.

Dwight shook his head. "No. Like I said, I just do the parties."

Karen and Quincy gave each other disapproving looks. Sasha couldn't have picked a worst candidate for the father of his grandchild.

"Dad, what's wrong?" Sasha asked.

"I guess I'm confused about where we went wrong as parents, because for you two to talk about having a child when you're still, for the most part, children yourselves is baffling to me."

"Man, I'm a grown man. I take care of mines. Please believe that." Dwight pounded on his chest.

Quincy wanted to break his face for having the audacity to place himself in the same category as Quincy. Quincy was a man because he made calculated decisions and also kept his responsibilities at the forefront of his life.

"How? How do you take care of yours?" Quincy asked.

Sasha came to her baby daddy's defense. "Dwight plans to be a producer."

"Well, there are a lot of people your age that want to become a producer. What are you going to do that is different?" Quincy replied.

"What do you mean?" Dwight asked.

"I mean, if God has blessed you with a gift, then it must be unique. So what makes you unique and different from everyone else?"

"I don't know," Dwight replied.

That answer disturbed Quincy in so many ways. *Imagine wanting to achieve something and not knowing the means by which to obtain it,* he thought. It was a psyche that was both foreign and unsettling to him.

"Sasha is a good girl, and she's going to be a great mother," Dwight said.

"I know she's a good girl and that she's going to be a great mother. Her mother and I raised her that way. The question is, what kind of a father are you going to be?" Quincy still could not wrap his head around the fact that they were talking to the father of Sasha's child. "Can you provide for a family on a DJ's salary?"

"No, but I'm going to go out and get it," Dwight said.

"You see, that's what troubles me," Quincy answered. "Because you have no vision, you'll do whatever it takes to obtain it. If you have no vision, you'll take short gains and cut corners. Without vision, there's self-destruction, or as the Word says, you'll perish."

Now Dwight seemed to be enjoying the chicken more than the conversation. Quincy never liked to preach, but what could he do when he saw someone who was lost?

"You got a lot to think about, and a short time in which to think about it, before this baby comes," Quincy said to both Dwight and himself.

"I think what my husband is trying to say . . . ," Karen stated.

"I'm not *trying* to say anything. I have said it in plain English," Quincy said.

Karen's eyes cut Quincy deep, but Quincy was not concerned with Karen's irritation.

"What I'm trying to say is that Sasha has a lot going for herself, and having a baby only makes her career goals more difficult," Quincy said.

"Well, I love Sasha very much, and I'm going to be there for her and for my child," Dwight said.

"Excuse me." Quincy had heard enough, so he got up and threw his napkin down on the table. It was a bitter pill for Quincy to swallow. He had failed as a parent, and given his past failings as a husband, the only true success he had known was his business.

Quincy entered the restroom and washed his hands under a gold faucet, but he did not know what dirt he was trying to get rid of. He was certain that it was more internal than external. If Sasha wanted to ruin her life, then so be it. Quincy was going to have to let her find out the hard way that life was not as sweet as he and Karen had made it for her over the years.

Quincy looked in the mirror. With a heavy burden placed squarely on his shoulders, he saw a man that was not equal to the task. He resisted the urge to look away, and instead, he faced his insecurities and his fears. Like he had done so many times before, he began to speak to them.

"God, you have given me the mind to build and rebuild. I've accomplished more than my father and grandfather. I have traveled the world and became a multimillionaire. I am a good husband and a great father, and I won't allow the mistakes of my child to cause me to sin. I will arise with confidence and strength and victory."

Another image was reflected in the mirror. It was of a man who had just finished using the restroom and had a perplexed look on his face.

"In times like these, you got to encourage yourself," Quincy said.

"I know that's the truth," the man said as he approached the sink next to Quincy and started to wash his hands.

Quincy dried his hands before he exited the restroom and made his way back to the dinner table, where, it appeared to Quincy, the conversation had moved on without him.

"Are you okay, baby?" Karen asked Quincy.

"Yeah, I'm fine. Something wasn't agreeing with me." Quincy took his seat.

"We were just talking, and I was telling Dwight about the men's retreat, and I think that it would be a good idea if he went with you," Karen announced.

"That's funny. I don't," Quincy replied.

"Daddy," Sasha said.

"I mean, this is a real serious thing. Men go to the retreat to seek guidance for their life," Quincy replied.

"That would be perfect for Dwight," Karen said.

Quincy wished that Karen would stop answering for Dwight. He also wished that she would stop forcing the issue about the men's retreat, but Quincy couldn't deny that Karen had a somewhat valid idea.

"I mean, if you are not doing anything . . ." Quincy was less than enthusiastic.

"Sure. I'm down." Dwight seemed more eager to join Quincy on his weekend excursion.

And with that, Quincy did not know if this meeting was a divine appointment or an utter embarrassment.

# Chapter Eleven

## Will

*The Eve of the Retreat . . .*

"What do you mean, you don't know where he is?" Will asked.

"He's gone. He's been gone for two days now," Will's mother said in between sobs.

For so long, Will's mother's emotions had lain dormant, due in part to her drug-induced state. For Will to witness his mother express her emotions was a shock, and he did not know how to react or handle the situation.

"Where's Dad?"

"He's out there somewhere, trying to hustle up some money."

*It figures. My father can't do right to save his life.*

"I don't want to lose my baby. Please find him."

His mother had ignored reality so much that to deal with it was unbearable.

"Look, Mom, when I find Josh, I'm not bringing him back here. If you want to see him, I will make arrangements, but I can't keep leaving my brother here. This isn't the environment for him."

"What are you talking about? He's my son."

"You think he's safe here?" Will made a calculated step toward his mother. "Look deep into your heart, and you know that I'm right and that this is no place for my brother to live. Dad is hardly even here, and what kind of an example does he set when he is here?"

Will's mother leaned back with a sadistic grin, as if she had been possessed and the demon that Will now spoke to was more amused than threatened. "Well, look at you! You're the man now. You think you know what's best? You think you're better than me? Well, you'll never be better than me, because I gave birth to you. I sat up in that foul-smelling hospital and pushed you out with pain, and there's no way you're better than me."

Will realized his posture was too aggressive and made his mother defensive. He took a seat on the couch next to her and allowed for the tension of the moment to settle down.

"You're right, Mom. You birthed me not out of love, but pain. Pain from the fact that your life revolves around waiting. Waiting for my father to be released, waiting for my father to come home, waiting for the government to send you a check, waiting and waiting. Nothing in your life has anything to do with you or what you want. You birthed me out of pain. For most of my life, that's all I knew, until I met Jesus and He taught me that even pain has a purpose." Saying the name of Jesus not only elicited a warm feeling in Will's stomach, but it also brought forth a lone tear in his mother's eye.

"I'm not better. I just know that I don't feel invisible anymore or empty or like there is no meaning to all of this. I'm trying to understand more than anything this new thing, and I know that with me my brother has a chance to change his life." Will's mother was silent, but he knew that she'd heard his every word. "I'm not the enemy, Mom. We both want the best for Josh. I just believe he has a better shot with me."

"Bring him back," Will's mother said as she removed a pack of cigarettes from her purse. She not only lit a cigarette but proceeded to smoke it in front of her daughter, who lay asleep in the playpen next to the TV.

Without another word, Will accepted his assignment from the queen of this household and proceeded toward the door. He had to find his brother, but first, he had to escape from here in one piece. Will peeked out the blinds next to the front door to see who was outside. There was a gathering of members from the Untouchables. Some he used to run with, and some Will had never seen before today.

Will was boxed into a corner. He did not want to leave his mother and sister alone, but he knew that his old crew would not harm them. He was the only one that they wanted. His bike parked out front must have tipped them off that he was there.

"What's wrong?" Will's mother asked.

"I can't go out the front. Hold on. Let me think of something."

Will knew he had to think fast. He had to figure out a way out of there and find his brother. His escape was first. Will pulled out his phone and sent a text message to the one friend that he could trust in this situation.

"Nobody's coming in here, are they?" Will's mother asked.

"I don't think so." Will looked outside again and saw that the group was growing restless, but they held their positions and did not advance. Will's cell phone gave him an alert that he had a new text message. His friend was on his way. Next, he had to figure out where Josh was.

# Chapter Twelve

## *Jamal*

Despite his vow to move out, Jamal continued to live with Chantel. He reasoned that with less than three months to go before his wedding day, it made no sense to move out of his apartment and get another place or to live in a hotel. Jamal had grown comfortable with his living arrangement, and since he and Chantel had agreed not to have sex until their wedding day, then maybe God's grace would watch over his household.

But each day Jamal grew weaker and more susceptible to temptation.

Chantel emerged from the bathroom located in the bedroom in nothing but a pink towel that smothered her figure-eight frame.

"I'm sorry," said Jamal, who stood in the middle of the bedroom. "I knew you were in the shower, but I thought—"

"It's okay." Chantel dried her hair with another pink towel as the sun peeked through the blinds and highlighted her skin.

Water sat on top of her flesh, with no rush to evaporate. Jamal could feel the tower of his willpower crumble.

"Where's Jamir?" Chantel asked.

"He's in his room, asleep," Jamal replied, and now that an opportunity had been established, all that remained was space.

Jamal feared rejection, but his desire screamed for him to discard pride and yield to indulgence. He crossed the room and took Chantel by the waist. Kissing her was like biting into a ripe honeydew melon, so sweet that he could go on for hours without stopping. Chantel did not hold back. She wrapped her arms around him, and her wet body and Jamal's hot body meshed. When Jamal's hands began to search the bottom of her towel, he felt a prick in his heart. The small wound made him face a major issue. He and Chantel were about to allow their passion for one another to cause them to make a mistake. Their passion had always been the source of their woes. Jamal put his head down, and Chantel went right on kissing his forehead.

"We can't," Jamal said as he took Chantel by her hands and clasped them together as in prayer.

"I know." Chantel broke free from Jamal's grip and proceeded to get dressed.

Overwhelmed, Jamal felt his knees give out, and he flopped down on the bed in complete surrender to the moment. He was confused about what he wanted, and that concerned him more than anything else.

"Let me ask you something. Do you think we're okay?" Chantel asked.

"Yeah, of course. Why?" Jamal asked.

"Sometimes I wonder if we're going to make it," Chantel said.

Jamal sat up on the bed and asked, "If you feel that way, then why do you want to get married?".

Chantel had her back turned to Jamal while she searched through the drawers for clothes. She turned to face Jamal, and a cloud took up residence in her eyes. Jamal could not tell what Chantel felt at the moment.

"When I was a little girl, I used to pray for the perfect man. When I got older, I prayed for the ideal man. You are what I prayed for, but since I've done a good job of making a mess of good things, I figure that it won't stop with you."

"I'm not going to disappoint you," Jamal said.

"You can't guarantee that." Chantel started to put on her clothes.

"You're right, I can't, but I know this. I love you, and for whatever it's worth, you weren't my ideal future wife, but you've become more than what I could ever pray for."

As they conversed in the bedroom, Jamal realized that living together without a covenant only blurred the lines. Jamal and Chantel had gotten comfortable, he and Chantel's relationship had lost it's edge. Love existed on the edge, and it was not meant for the complacent, but for the compassionate.

"Listen, I'm going to go stay with a friend for a little while." Jamal felt like a coward. He couldn't look at Chantel as he spoke. "Just until the wedding."

"I don't know what to say." Chantel got in Jamal's face. "First, you postpone the wedding, and now you're moving out. Just think about it, J, and try to see it from my point of view. Would you trust the person you were going to marry when every time you looked up, they seemed to be pushing you away?"

"It's not even like that!"

Chantel slipped out of her towel and into a pair of jean shorts and a black tank top. "You can do whatever you want. Just know that I won't be surprised if I get that call saying that the wedding is off!"

"Whatever." Jamal conceded that he wasn't going to win this argument, so he gave Chantel a dismissive wave and went into the living room. Chantel followed

Jamal out of the bedroom, but she made her way toward Jamir's room.

Jamal went into the closet near the front door and pulled out his duffel bag. Even though Jamal knew he was doing the right thing, at the same time he felt stupid. That proved that a person could do the right thing and still feel stupid. He went back into his bedroom and started to pack.

Jamal was about to call Will and ask to stay with him until the wedding when he got a text message from Will. It stated that he needed Jamal's help. Jamal feared that his friend was in serious danger since Will had asked Jamal to pick him up in the alley of his old apartment. Jamal could think about the details later, but he needed to leave now. Jamal texted Will back, letting him know that he was on his way. He had snatched the car keys off his counter and was making a beeline to the door when Chantel emerged with Jamir in her arms.

"Where you going?" Chantel asked as she put Jamir on the floor. Jamir ran over to a corner of the living room, where he pulled out a toy car and started to play with it.

"I got to go pick Will up. I'll be right back."

Chantel did not respond. She just looked at Jamal's duffel bag. Finally, she said, "Are we going to talk before you leave?"

"Baby, I can't do this right now. We've agreed that this is the right thing."

"No, you made a decision, and I guess if I'm going to be a Christian woman, I got to live with you putting your foot down."

Jamal prayed that whatever tight spot Will was in, he could hold on for just one moment. "Chantel, I love you, but I'm not going to be married without God's covering. We won't make it."

"Do you know how hard it was for me to tell everyone that we were not getting married in September, but in December instead? Do you know I got family and friends telling me that I'm stupid for waiting? Now you want to move out. I don't know if I can take too much more of this."

Jamal did not have time for this, but at the same time he could not have his fiancée thinking that she was a fool. "Do *you* think you're foolish for waiting for me?"

"No, but I just wonder why there are so many obstacles in our way if this is really meant to happen."

Jamal wondered the same thing. It seemed like the more he and Chantel tried to build a life together, the more difficult it became. "I love you, and I want this to work."

"I guess you're not the only one who has a lot to think about this weekend." Chantel walked over to Jamir. "Go get your friend."

Jamal did not head out the door. Instead, he walked over to Jamir and gave him a kiss on the forehead. He took Chantel by the hand and gave her a kiss too. "I love you, and we're going to be okay."

"I love you too." Chantel gave Jamal a kiss on the cheek.

Jamal allowed the taste of Chantel's lips on his to linger as he sprinted out the door to his friend's aid.


"You hate me, don't you?" Will's mother asked in such a low tone, Will wondered if he was meant to hear her question.

"I don't hate you." Will took another peek out the window. "I just don't understand."

"Understand what?"

"How two people could have children and not really care about them. If you just wanted it to be you and Dad, then there's pills for that."

"You think you know everything. That Bible has made you as ignorant as ever."

Will moved away from the window and had a seat. "Help me understand."

"You won't." Will's mother leaned back on the couch. "You're just as stubborn as your father."

"Try!"

A second turned into a long moment, and in between there were no words spoken. Then Will's mother sat forward and took a drag of what was left of her cigarette. She allowed both the smoke and a tear to escape. "The moment you were born, you were so precious that I knew that Odell and I didn't deserve you. I knew that we would find a way to screw it up somehow. I hated myself because of you. I knew I wasn't good enough, so what was the point in trying?"

"You didn't have to have me."

The statement caused Carroll to shake like she had chills. "I don't believe in killing no babies."

"No, you just believe in leaving them defenseless and uncared for."

"What do you want me to say? Huh! Sorry? I'm sorry for ruining your life."

"I don't know. I don't know what I want you to say. All I know is that I got a lot of anger and bitterness toward you that I'm trying to deal with."

"The Bible talks about forgiveness."

"Yeah, and you and I know that's easier said than done. I could say that I forgive you, but that wouldn't be true. The truth is forgiveness is a process, and I'm not ready to forgive you." Will turned away from his mother, because his words felt like razors cutting at his throat.

"What does that say about your newfound faith if you can't even forgive your own mother for the wrong I've done?"

"It says God is still working on me, but at least I know where my broken places are. For years I blamed my father for not being there, but the truth is you weren't there, either. The only difference is Pop was in a small prison cell. You were right in this living room, withdrawn."

"Talk to me in five years, when you've had enough disappointments, and see if you don't turn out withdrawn."

"Mom, I don't hate you. I love you, and I want to forgive you, but it's hard letting go when you don't know what to do after you let go."

How to let go? That was something that Will had struggled with for the past year. Christ wanted him to lay his burdens aside, but some burdens were so heavy that Will was afraid he would collapse if he let them go.

Will's phone sounded with another text message alert. Jamal was outside in the alley, just as Will had instructed.

"Listen, Mom. I got to go. I'll call you when I get Josh safely back to my place."

Will's mother did not respond. It was as if the whole conversation that had just transpired was a figment of Will's imagination.

Will made his way to his old room, which he used to share with Joshua. It had a window that would pop off real easy. This was a time when Will wished his parents' apartment had a back door. There was a narrow space between the apartment building and a barbwire fence. Will would have to drop down to the closed black Dumpster without being hurt. The impact of Will's fall would alert his former gang members to his presence.

Without hesitation, Will would have to make his way down the narrow pathway to the alley where he'd told Jamal to park.

Will wasted no time at all. He popped off the window, leaned it against the wall, climbed up through the open space, and positioned himself to drop down. Will jumped, and his feet absorbed the impact of a two-story drop onto concrete. As soon as Will's equilibrium was reestablished, he dashed toward the silver Civic with factory-tinted windows. He had a small window of time to make it to the car without being spotted.

# Chapter Thirteen

## *Chauncey*

"She said she was coming?" Brother Mitchell said from his hospital bed.

That was the only statement Brother Mitchell uttered that did not reflect the anguish he suffered from lymphoma. Chauncey sat beside Brother Mitchell and wondered how the nurses were able to get so many injections and tubes into such a frail body.

"She said she was coming," Chauncey said, but he knew that Brother Mitchell's ex-wife had been saying that she was coming to see her terminally ill ex-husband for two months now. She had yet to make good on her promise.

"I don't know what I'll do if I leave here before I get to see my Patricia." Brother Mitchell swallowed hard, and tears slipped from his eyes.

"Don't get yourself worked up, Brother Mitchell. You don't know what God has in store for you."

"I do know. I've seen it in my dreams. God is so awesome, but my father told me a long time ago that a man should try to settle all his accounts before he goes home. I made peace with everyone but my Patricia," Brother Mitchell said.

After the death of Henry, Chauncey thought that it would be therapeutic for him to join the healing ministry at church. He figured that the best way to deal with not being there for his brother in the end was to be there for others as they made their transition. Of course, the healing ministry had different aspects, but Chauncey made it a point to visit those who did not have much time left. In the past six months he had learned more from people who were at the end of their life than he had learned in all of his thirty-eight years.

"Did I tell you about the sixty-seven Mustang?" Brother Mitchell asked.

"What about it?" Chauncey asked, even though he had heard about the Mustang every day for the past month. He figured that elderly people remembered only a few precious moments. Brother Mitchell's was a '67 Mustang, which he used to take his then bride, Patricia, for rides in.

"I had this sixty-seven Mustang. It was candy-apple red with a white leather interior. I used to take Patricia for a ride, and she would get scared because I drove too fast. I used to tell her they didn't build Mustangs to go slow."

Chauncey and Brother Mitchell enjoyed a chuckle. Chauncey always seemed to find both humor in Mitchell's story and concern, because it took a lot out of Mitchell to tell it.

"We'd go to the drive-in and not even remember the movie that we saw." Mitchell turned away from Chauncey, as if he was lost in thought. "Why couldn't that be enough? Why?"

Brother Mitchell's rhetorical question referred to the woman whom he would eventually leave Patricia for and thus begin the second of three failed marriages. Patricia remained the woman whom he regretted leaving the most, and that was why it was so essential for Mitchell to make things right with her.

"Get some sleep, Brother Mitchell. She'll be here soon enough," Chauncey said.

Even with the disease tearing through his body without mercy, Mitchell was still able to look at Chauncey and convey that he did not believe the good deacon.

"I'll see you tomorrow," Chauncey said as he stood up to walk out.

"You can't promise that," Mitchell replied.

Chauncey prayed over Mitchell, as he'd done since he first started visiting him, and then walked out of the room. Chauncey walked down the hall with a spirit of heaviness in his heart. He couldn't believe that in some ways, he envied Brother Mitchell. Chauncey would not wish any kind of disease on even his worst enemy, but Brother Mitchell had experienced something that still remained both elusive and obscure to Chauncey: true love.

Even though Brother Mitchell was responsible for the collapse of his marriage, Chauncey still marveled at how Mitchell recognized who his true love was and what true love meant. Throughout his life, Chauncey had less than a handful of girlfriends, and he used the term *girlfriends* loosely. In actuality he'd dated only a couple of women for a short time, and the thought of never having a girlfriend was too much for Chauncey to bear. Two things that weighed heavily on Chauncey's heart were that Brother Mitchell might die while waiting for his ex-wife to show up and that Chauncey might die without anyone to call on.

He arrived at the elevator and watched as it counted down to his floor. He then looked at a distorted image of himself in the still mirrored doors when the elevator arrived. Fittingly enough, the steel doors split open and so did Chauncey's image.

# Chapter Fourteen

## *Will*

"This is a bad idea," Will said from the passenger seat.

"Oh yeah? And driving out here all by yourself is a brilliant idea? Listen, I don't want to spend this drive arguing over whose plan is dumber. That's like arguing over which handcuffs feel more comfortable," Jamal said.

Will leaned back in his seat and stared at the backdrop of the city. At night the city of Los Angeles could be awe-inspiring. Skyscrapers, the Staples Center, a mountain range that led into the valley. Will understood the allure of the city and why so many came to try their hand at stardom. But there were some areas that not even Los Angeles's skyline could illuminate. West of the 110 freeway lay blocks of abandoned buildings, which were emblematic of an impoverished landscape.

Will still had a few contacts from his old stomping grounds that knew everything that went down with the Untouchables. Joshua and his crew were making noise around town, Will discovered. That was the problem with today's gangsters: they talked too much. Not only was his brother a member of the Untouchables, but he had also assumed Will's old responsibility of stealing cars. Josh wanted to be like Will, but he was not. Joshua and his crew were being sloppy. Will detested his old life, but he at least had a little more polish in his time as a car thief.

He got word that Joshua and his crew were at a house party. Will found out that Joshua spent a lot of time at the Crenshaw mall. The reason why Joshua hung out so far from his home was beyond comprehension. Will learned that some girls who Joshua had met at the mall had invited Joshua and his crew to the party. That only added to his brother's foolish thinking. He was a long ways from home and did not understand the territory. Will had to get him back.

Will's thoughts switched from his brother to the conversation he had had earlier with his mother. Will had many regrets in his life, and among them was his relationship with his parents and his failure at being a good role model for his brother. Joshua had grown up watching Will handle business, make money, and collect respect. How naive of Will to believe that his one year of being saved would cause Joshua to abandon his present course.

"Let me ask you something." Will turned to a focused Jamal.

"What's up?"

"Do you believe the Bible when it says that the sins of a father affect several generations?"

"Yes, but I also believe that the generational curse ends when someone takes a stand and says, 'Enough.'"

Will prayed that he would be strong enough to take a stand and protect his family. He didn't want to lose his brother, but Joshua had gotten entangled in a web that only God could pull him out of.

"Listen, J, you know what the get down is at these functions? Nothing good goes down."

"I know," Jamal said.

"You know? What do you mean, you know?"

"I've attended so many wakes that resulted from an out-of-control party."

"Man, you got everything going for you. You're about to get married," Will said.

"Proverbs seventeen, seventeen. 'A friend loves at all times, and a brother is born for adversity.' It's easy to be your friend when we're shooting pool, chopping it up. But here right now is where you need me the most."

They arrived at a green and white flat that faced the street. The sidewalk was packed with guys drinking and smoking. Will knew this was the place, because his muscles started to tighten up. Jamal parked across the street, in front of a barbershop. They had to be quick. This was not a neighborhood in which to park a luxury car.

"Last chance." Will did not even turn around to look at Jamal.

"I'm not going home, nor am I going in there without a word of prayer." Jamal bowed his head, and Will followed suit. "Lord, don't let us get shot or killed. Amen!"

"Amen!"

The two men exited the car and jogged across the street, avoiding oncoming traffic on the four-lane street. They made their way past the guys standing in the front yard. The backyard was accessible through a narrow walkway that had piles of junk lined up along the sides. The junk was indiscernible at night.

The junk impeded Will's progress. As he drew closer to the music, he heard Chris Brown's latest song blasting from speakers. Teenagers were grinding their glistening bodies against each other. In October the nights were cooler, but the warmth of the summer still lingered. But nothing could beat the heat that existed between the boys that danced with the girls and the girls that ground against each other. Will searched for

Joshua on the dance floor, but he didn't find him. Will looked along the walls, and all he saw were different groups of guys huddled together, plotting, waiting for something to happen next.

"We got to find Josh, quickly," Will said, to which Jamal nodded in agreement.

The danger element came from the guys who were not dancing and instead had come to the party to drink, smoke, and cause mayhem. Will found his brother in the midst of those intent on doing the third thing. He and his two friends sat in chairs, while three girls his brother's age grind up against them.

"That's right, Li-Li. Do like how Momma showed you," a middle-aged woman said, encouraging a girl, whom Will presumed was her daughter, to continue to grind against his brother.

Joshua broke out a knot of money, and he started to sprinkle the air with it as the girl in return swerved her butt. Joshua also took sips of a drink from a red plastic cup. Will did not want to speculate on what they had done to earn the money. Instead, he made a beeline to his brother and snatched him up by his arm.

"Let's go," Will ordered Joshua.

"Come on, man. Stop hating," Joshua snapped. He fought to regain control of his arm.

"And I ain't repeating myself, neither." Will reestablished his grip on Joshua.

"You doing extras!" said the young girl who was grinding on Joshua.

"You doing the most. Where your momma at?" Jamal asked the girl.

"Right there." The girl pointed to the voluptuous woman who had cheered her on moments before. Now the woman was on the dance floor, shaking her massive butt.

"Dang!" Jamal, Will, and Joshua said in unison.

"Come on. I'm trying to get a rub up on something." Joshua turned to the side and hurled.

Will turned his attention to the contents of Joshua's cup. He snatched the cup away from his brother and spilled some of the drink on his hand.

"Come on, bro," Joshua slurred.

Will lifted the cup to his nose and smelled the strong liquid. He knew exactly what it was, a mixture of different types of alcohol and the energy drink Four Loko, otherwise known as FoLo and "blackout in a can." Four Loko had four main ingredients: alcohol and the stimulants caffeine, taurine, and guarana. It came in 6 percent and 12.5 percent alcohol. Will would ring his brother's neck later, but first he had to get him out of there.

"Our mom is at home, worried sick about you. I'm taking you home now," Will said. He didn't say another word.

He grabbed Joshua and made his way toward the front.

"Josh, where you going?" Peanut, Josh's friend, asked.

"Home, and if you want a ride, you better come with me," Will said as he continued to walk toward the front. Will dragged Joshua by his arm to the front yard.

"Let me go," Joshua snapped, attracting the attention of the guys up front.

"Hey, if little man says let him go, then let him go or else," one guy said.

The man dwarfed Will, but that did not scare him. The man had a half-empty bottle of gin in his hand, and that did not bother Will, either. What bothered Will was that between him and Jamal's car were three drunken gangsters and a busy four-lane street. Even if they got past the guys, Will wondered how they would get away. Out of his peripheral vision he saw Jamal trying to figure out the schematics himself.

"Come on, brother. We're just trying to take our little brothers home before it gets too late," Jamal said, trying the Christian approach.

That did not move the guy.

"Dude, we ain't got a problem with you, so step aside." Will said, trying the street approach.

The guy refused to move, so Will moved him with a fist to the guy's stomach. Jamal pushed the second guy into the third guy, which cleared a way for them to escape. They ran across the street. Joshua and his friend were ahead of them, but oncoming traffic caused the boys to zigzag. Will felt a sudden injection of fear, for he did not know how they were going to survive the scene. Just then, guns started to fire.

Will pulled ahead of Joshua and Peanut in the footrace to the car. Between the cars that sped toward them and screeched to a sudden halt and the bullets that whisked by, Will doubted his chances of survival were high. He didn't hear any screams, so he assumed that no one had been hit, but the car still seemed too far away to get to. Even if they made it to the car, getting in it and getting away seemed like a near impossibility. Will reached the car first, but it was no good, because he did not have the keys.

"Will?"

Will turned around to see Jamal toss him the car keys. Will caught the keys and unlocked the car. By the time Will got into the car and turned on the ignition, Jamal, Joshua and Peanut were at the car, and the two-way traffic impeded the gunmen's progress enough to allow Will and the others to escape. Will did not wait for his door to close before driving off. He sped up the street and ran a red light.

"God, I hope we don't get stopped by the pos," Jamal said.

"We'll keep going up Western until we get to Florence. Then we'll get on the one-ten from there," Will announced.

Will eyed the speedometer. Between the different notorious gangs that occupied this area of West Los Angeles and the infamous LAPD, Will could not afford to get stopped on their journey back to Long Beach. Will had advised Jamal to take his Honda Civic and leave the Camaro, but the Camaro's three hundred horsepower would have come in handy. Will made a sharp left on Florence and started to relax, but not too much. There was still a lot of territory to cover between Florence and Long Beach.

"We're good, Will. Slow this bad boy down," Jamal said while looking through the passenger-side mirror.

Will nodded. "Cool. I just want to get out of here."

"I don't feel so good, bro," Joshua said.

"Josh, you throw up in my car and you're walking home," Jamal whined.

"Josh, I just got one question. How stupid are you to go to a party where nobody knows you?" Will said.

Joshua didn't reply.

Will shook his head. "And another thing, you're too darn small to be drinking Four Loko. That stuff will put you on your back."

"That stuff will kill you," Jamal added.

"A'ight, man. I only got one mother," Joshua snapped.

Will looked at his brother in the rearview mirror. Joshua rubbed his stomach, and it was clear to Will that his little brother was in intense discomfort. His friend Peanut was asleep, which meant that the blackout can had lived up to its name.

"I ain't your mother. I'm your brother, which means I can smack some sense into you."

"Pull over," Joshua said in anguish.

They were a block away from the freeway, but Will knew that his brother couldn't wait that long. Will pulled over to the sidewalk, and Jamal opened the door for Joshua to lean out. Joshua leaned out and started to hurl.

"Watch it!" Jamal said.

"Don't worry, J. I'll pay to get it detailed," Will said.

"You don't make enough. Don't worry about it."

Will took offense at Jamal's jab. He knew that his friend did not mean to insult him, but Will still was offended that Jamal would look down on his financial situation. Joshua finished throwing up and leaned back into the car and lay back with his head resting on the car seat.

Relief set in when Will reached the freeway and cruised along, with very few cars to hinder his progress. The silver Civic disappeared in the cloak of the night.

"Well, that was eventful," Jamal said.

"J, I'm so sorry, man. I didn't want you to get mixed up in my brother's mess," Will told him.

"Don't worry about it. I wish I had a brother like you that was willing to keep me out of trouble."

Amber and red lights flashed, along with a bright light. Being shot at caused Will to lose sight of how fast he was going.

"Just be cool, Will, and pull over." Jamal did not take his eyes off the cop car behind them as he gazed in the side mirror.

By now Joshua was asleep, along with Peanut, but not for long, and Lord knows, they smelled like a liquor store.

"Joshua, Peanut, wake up!" Will called, and he moved from the far left lane toward the far right lane as the black-and-white squad car stalked him.

"What, man?" Jamal asked.

"The pos is on us. You ain't got nothing on you, do you?" Will yelled.

"Naw, man," Peanut said while rubbing his head.

Will prayed that there were not any drugs or unregistered weapons on his brother and his brother's friend. "Don't lie!" Will said.

"He said no," Joshua snapped.

Will pulled the car into the turnout lane, and the police car pulled up behind him with its lights still flashing.

"How fast was I going?" Will asked Jamal.

"I don't know, I wasn't paying attention. It couldn't have been that fast, though."

"All your papers are straight?" Will said.

"Of course, insurance and everything," Jamal said as he went into his glove compartment and searched for his papers.

The familiar sound of the window being tapped only twisted Will's stomach more. Will rolled down the window and was greeted by a bright flashlight.

"License and registration," the officer said.

Jamal handed over his information to Will, and Will handed the information to the officer.

"You know how fast you were going?" the officer said while examining Jamal's license.

"I'm sorry, Officer. I'm just trying to get home." Will smiled.

"Have you been drinking?" the officer asked.

"No, sir," Will said.

"It sure smells like it." The officer put the flashlight down to get a good look at Will and his passengers.

The officer's skin was as black as Will's, but he gave a sadistic smile as he scanned the interior of the car. He turned his flashlight to Will. "Have I seen you before?"

"Probably not. I don't be in this area often," Will said.

"Naw, I think you're from forties or maybe sixties," the officer responded. "Yeah you're from one of these gangs around here. I bet if I run your name, I'll come up with all kinds of interesting things."

"Naw, man. I'm just trying to get home." Will could feel himself losing control. His anger had grown, and he could only transfer it to the steering wheel he gripped.

"Hey! Wake up!" The officer flashed his light on Joshua and Peanut. "Where you from? Huh? What are your gang names?"

Will prayed that Joshua and Peanut would use wisdom and would not use this as an opportunity to show their ignorance

"We ain't from nowhere," Joshua said.

"It's past curfew. Y'all shouldn't even be out!" the officer said.

"I'm his brother. I'm trying to get him home," Will interjected.

The officer started making a sniffing gesture. He knew what the car smelled like, and Will feared that he and his brother might end up in handcuffs.

"You know it's illegal for underage minors to consume alcohol?" the officer quizzed.

"I'm aware." At this point, Will was done with the games. *Let the officer do what he wants to do.*

Will waited for the officer to ask him to step outside the car. Instead, the police officer started to write a ticket.

"Watch the speed, and get home safe." The officer handed Will the ticket.

Will waited until the officer left to let out a sigh of relief. He waited until the squad car pulled away before he resumed his journey home.

"I don't know if I can go tomorrow to this retreat, J." Will did not take his eyes off the road.

"You need to go, just like I do," Jamal replied.

"My mind is cloudy right now. I won't be able to focus. I don't know. I got to protect my brother." Will looked in the rearview at Josh, who had nodded off again. He wondered if he could protect his brother.

# Chapter Fifteen

## *Jamal*

After a wild night last night, Jamal just wanted to check in to his hotel and relax before the start of the retreat. This retreat was different from last year's, and Jamal was in a different place. The last thing Jamal expected was to be summoned by Pastor Dawkins to come to his hotel room at once. Having to appear before Pastor Dawkins was a lot like being sent to the principal's office for misbehavior. As Jamal made his way to Pastor Dawkins's hotel room, he tried to figure out the reason Pastor Dawkins wanted to see him. The man walked so strongly in the Holy Spirit that maybe he knew about his and Chantel's living situation. Anxiety filled Jamal before he reached the pastor's door. He knocked on the door, and the hollow sound the oak made when it came in contact with Jamal's fist was unnerving.

Moments later Pastor Dawkins opened the door. He was alone, which was unusual. Pastor Dawkins usually traveled with his armor bearers. Pastor Dawkins's attire was toned down considerably. Jamal found his pastor in just a black T-shirt and sweats.

"Mighty man of God, please come in." Pastor Dawkins motioned for Jamal to come inside.

"God bless you, Pastor." Jamal felt more inclined to walk in after the greeting.

"Care for one?" Pastor extended a can of honey-roasted peanuts to Jamal.

"No, thank you, Pastor."

Pastor Dawkins proceed to grab a fistful of peanuts and pop them into his mouth in clusters.

"So what's up, Pastor?" Jamal asked as he took a seat on the edge of the bed.

"Well, I just wanted to get a chance to talk with you and see how everything is going."

"Everything is going well, Pastor. How is everything with you?"

"Good. The big day is coming?"

"Yeah, my last retreat as a single man." Jamal rubbed his hands on his knees.

"Pastor Brown tells me that things are going well with you and Chantel."

"I don't see how."

"How so?" Pastor Dawkins's face turned sour.

"Well, it seems like the more we go to counseling, the more we argue and the more areas that we see we need to work on."

Pastor Dawkins started to laugh, which led him to cough, as a result of the fact that he was still eating peanuts.

"What?" Jamal could not help but laugh at the sight of his pastor.

"That's good. There's nothing wrong with disagreements. Most couples wait until they have already married to discover their differences, and by then it's too late." Pastor Dawkins sat the can of peanuts down on the dresser. He had a seat on the edge of his bed, alongside Jamal.

"I guess you're right."

"The world sees marriage as an act of two people, a man and a woman, and in this day and age, a woman and a woman and a man and a man. But every believer has to go into marriage knowing that there is a third entity, and that's God. Let God be the mediator at times when you and Chantel have differences."

Jamal felt blessed to be in the presence of Pastor Dawkins. Since the last retreat he had learned not to place men of God on too high a pedestal. He remained respectful, but he understood that in the end a man of God was still a man and was capable of falling flat on his face.

"Did Pastor Brown tell you about Chantel and me living together?"

"He did, and I'm a little disappointed in you."

"But, Pastor, when Chantel lost her job, it was hard on her, and I can't leave my future wife and son out in the cold."

"I understand, but your mind is supposed to be dwelling on heavenly things. You know that before you was even born, God had already worked out your life, Chantel's life, and Jamir's. Don't let the enemy cause you to second-guess that."

Jamal did not disagree with Pastor Dawkins, and he knew that his advice was scripturally based and sound, but it was hard for Jamal to walk by faith when his fiancée was struggling. It was in his nature to want to help.

"Well, I moved out. I'm staying with Will until the wedding. I just want to do the right thing."

Pastor Dawkins flashed a smile, as if Jamal had guessed the right answer to the final question on a game show.

"What?" Jamal asked.

"It's not easy doing the right thing, but God is faithful and nothing escapes Him," Pastor Dawkins said.

"There are just so many temptations out there that it's hard. I mean, I got a new boss that is bad, beautiful, smart, and a Christian. Sometimes she makes me question my choices. I don't know how you did it, Pastor, being single for as long as you were."

"Same way you are doing it, by the grace of God. I can't begin to count the times I spent counseling women that I wanted to be with. But God always reminded me that I had a higher calling and purpose. If you want to be a man of honor and integrity, then you're going to have to live and breathe it every day of your life. You are great man, Jamal, and there's a light on the inside of you that will draw plenty of attractive women toward you. Don't use the light God placed inside of you for the profit of the flesh."

Pastor Dawkins's last sentence stuck with Jamal. A lot of women at the job flirted with him, and though Jamal never addressed the women's advances, he knew that his female coworkers were infatuated with the ideal of him rather than with him as a person. He was the example that proved that not all men were dogs and that there were men who chose to stay and assume an active role model in their child's life. There was another side to Jamal that was deeply flawed. That side would turn the women at his job away, but not Chantel. She loved Jamal regardless of his faults.

"The reason why I called you in here is that I want you to sit in on the married men workshops," Pastor Dawkins informed him.

Jamal did not know if he should be honored or concerned. Joining the married men's group and not being married was the same as joining a team without signing a contract. Christian men had the same responsibilities as non-Christian men, only a married Christian man turned to his faith first and foremost whenever trouble would arise. At least in theory that was what he was supposed to do.

"I don't know about that," Jamal said.

"I think it would be helpful for you to see some of the challenges a married man faces on a daily basis. It will help you to be strong."

Jamal did not have to go far to see the challenges that a married man faced. His father was a model of how not to handle a marriage. He was rude, over-bearing, a womanizer, and Jamal grew up feeling so self-conscious, believing that if his father didn't yell and complain, then that meant that Jamal had done something right. He was not interested in being put in a room full of men that resembled his father. Of course, his father was not a man of faith. His wisdom and principles could be found in the bottom of a bottle. These men were believers, so in theory they should be different.

# Chapter Sixteen

## *Quincy*

Quincy would rather eat the wallpaper than spend another minute in the hotel room with Dwight. He thought about running over to the bed to strangle him for single-handedly derailing the future of his baby girl. This young man was brash and arrogant for no reason. Nothing existed in his cognitive, emotional, and spiritual bank that screamed success. Dwight personified the mentality of his generation. They were all proud of being cowards and were afraid to grow up. Quincy was disappointed in his daughter for both her actions and her choice of men, but he was not without hope that Dwight might in fact, want to be a good father.

"Man, thanks for getting me here," Dwight said.

"Let me help you out. This weekend is not about you getting closer to me. This is about you trying to see what God has for you."

"I know what God wants for my life," Dwight said without hesitation. "He wants me to be a rapper and a producer."

Dwight's comments provoked laughter from Quincy. If he had a nickel for every time he'd heard about someone's rap dream, he could stack one-dollar bills as high as the Empire State Building.

"Do you have a bank account?"

"No!"

"And how do you expect to build an empire without a bank account?" Quincy asked.

"Sasha told me that you started your company from nothing."

"But I had the wherewithal to not let anybody tell me nothing. You can't deny me anything that I want in this life. I refuse to lose. Do you have that kind of drive in you?"

"Yeah," Dwight said after he shrugged his shoulders.

Quincy tossed a magazine on the bed in frustration. He would need a bulldozer and ten years to plow through all the backward thinking.

"Can you be an individual?" Quincy asked.

"I *am* an individual." Dwight stood up and assumed a defensive stance.

"Watch yourself. I don't take boxing classes just to work up a sweat."

"Look, dude!"

"I'm not your dude!"

"Man, why are you always on my head?"

"Because you're about to be a father, and more importantly, you're about to be a father to my grandchild. Because my baby girl is becoming a mother before she even learned how to become a woman. That's why I'm on your head. You're lucky my foot is not . . ." Quincy grabbed at the air to try to regain control of his emotions.

A knock on the door seemed more ominous than usual.

"Q, it's Jamal and Chauncey. Open up."

Quincy opened the door and felt relief to find his brethren on the other side.

"What's up?" Quincy said as he leaned against the door.

"Denny's is still opened," Jamal informed him.

"Forget about it. I'm not going to Denny's," Quincy said.

"Come on. You know Chauncey is going to go crazy if he can't get any food."

Quincy laughed at the sight of Chauncey rubbing his belly. 'No, I'm not going. I don't care what you say. I'm not going to Denny's!"

Later on at Denny's, Quincy, Jamal, Chauncey, and Dwight gathered together and shared unforgettable moments from last year's retreat. Of course, Quincy would never forget the issues with the raccoons and Will with a gun.

"You mean to tell me that dude broke out a gun and started shooting?" Dwight asked.

"Yeah, and the raccoons scattered everywhere," Jamal said as he wiped the tears from his eyes.

"The pastor did not know how to approach him. He just assumed that Will had caps," Quincy added.

The eyes of everyone at the table were red from laughing. With time the laughter stopped, and silence took over for a brief moment.

"So, Dwight, are you ready for tomorrow?" Chauncey asked.

"I mean, I guess. This whole thing is overwhelming," Dwight said.

"Don't worry, young man of God. God will see you through," Chauncey said.

Quincy allowed his dull butter knife to spin around on top of the table. He knew his boys meant well, but he still felt a bit betrayed by the fact that they were not upset and were not reading Dwight the riot act.

Quincy finally spoke to Dwight. "Let me ask you something. What went through your mind when she finally told you?"

"What do you mean?" Dwight asked.

"You know exactly what I mean. Don't beat around the bush."

"I mean, I love Sasha and everything, but when she told me, I already knew and thought it was just my luck. Just when I was about to start getting things together, this goes and happens."

After Dwight delivered his statement, Quincy wished that he could transform his simple butter knife into a Ginsu. This would happen right after Sasha had graduated at the top of her class. Right when she was on track for a career as a pediatrician, with aspirations to help children in a third world country. "I believe that's more important than becoming the next Will.i.am."

"Wait a minute, Brother Page. It's not fair to just beat up on the boy like that," Chauncey said.

"C, I suggest you pull your nose up out of this business," Quincy replied.

"Is that the mind of Christ? You talk to your own brother like that. What do you think Apostle Paul would say?" Chauncey asked.

"Apostle Paul never had kids, and last time I checked, premarital sex was a sin," Quincy said.

"But we're all human." Chauncey shook his finger at Quincy.

"C, since when did you become the poster child for grace and mercy?"

"But I feel Deacon on this one, Q," Jamal interjected. "Hear the man out. That's the only way you're going to get any understanding and peace out of the situation."

Quincy did not respond directly to Jamal's point. Instead, he gave Dwight a head nod, to signal that he could continue with his explanation.

"I'm just saying, you know . . . I don't know how this happened," Dwight said.

Quincy dropped his hand like a gavel onto the table. Jamal let out a smirk and started to rub Quincy's shoulders to calm him down.

"Yeah, there are only a few ways it can happen," Jamal said.

Dwight shook his head. "But I'm saying that we're both adults, and I know I kept it wrapped up, and so how Sasha ended up pregnant, I don't know."

"Look, Dwight, my daughter bears as much responsibility for this situation as you do, but to suggest that my daughter wanted to get pregnant on purpose is ridiculous!"

"I'm just saying." Dwight started to pound his fist into his hand. "I ain't trying to have no babies, and I thought she was the same way! And what's with these *Law & Order* interrogations?"

"So now you're being belligerent?" Quincy asked.

"What does that mean?" Dwight retorted.

Quincy motioned in a way that indicated he was about to hop over the table and strangle Dwight, but Jamal held him back. "Easy, Q. We're just trying to talk things out." He looked Dwight in the eye. "Listen, Dwight, I understand that for you and Sasha, it was nothing serious, but having a baby is a real serious thing, and Q just wants to know that you're ready for the responsibility," Jamal said.

"And might I suggest, Brother Dwight, that you consider giving yourself over to the Lord and doing some research into laser surgery for all those ungodly tattoos," Chauncey said, to the puzzlement of everyone at the table.

Quincy gripped the knife harder. "You can make a choice to walk away right now and never see your kid. You would never have to deal with your kid's tears. Sasha has made a choice to have the baby. That is not something she can walk away from." Quincy dropped the knife, and it made a chiming sound. He wanted to go back to his room before he ended up committing a crime.

"What's good, fellas?" Will entered the restaurant with his brother.

"Hey, man, you made it." Jamal gave Will a fist pound.

"I figured this is the safest place to be right now. I decided to bring my brother with me," Will said.

"How did you know we were here?" Quincy asked.

"I stopped by the hotel and didn't see you guys, so I made a guess that you guys were over here getting something to eat."

Chauncey looked at Will, a little confused. "But, Brother Will, your brother is too young to be here."

"Don't worry, C. He's going to be in my room, getting caught up on some much-needed schoolwork."

A wry smile crept over Quincy's mouth as Will sized up Dwight. He knew that Will could spot an unsavory character from a mile away. He knew that if Dwight was hiding anything, Will would be able to spot it.

"What up, man?" Will said.

"Dwight." Dwight gave Will a fist bump.

"Dwight came here with Quincy. He's trying to see what this weekend is all about," Chauncey said.

Will nodded. "That's good. I came here a year ago, and it changed my life. I love these guys as if they were my own flesh and blood."

"Good, good! That's what's up!" Dwight replied.

"Have a seat, Joshua, and order some food," Will said.

Joshua had a seat and picked up a menu and started to thumb through it.

"How are you?" Quincy asked Will.

"I'm okay. Just trying to maintain while chasing this one around." Will pointed to his brother.

"Have you given that lawyer I referred you to a call?" Quincy asked.

"I did. She told me that I'm in for an uphill battle, trying to get my brother. I'm going to try to do it without getting the courts involved."

"Well, we will be praying for you that everything works out," Jamal said.

The waitress came, and Joshua ordered a meal, while Will ordered just a cup of coffee.

"So what you been talking about?" Will asked.

"We've been talking about this situation that Dwight has caused and how my so-called friends are taking his side," Quincy said.

"We're not taking sides. Come on, man. Don't be sensitive." Jamal gave Quincy a friendly tap on the shoulder, and Quincy batted Jamal's hand away with the back of his arm.

"I'm not being sensitive. My family is in crisis, and you guys don't know how hard it is for me to be here with this clown."

"Man, you ain't going to be disrespecting me, for real," Dwight said.

"I wish you would. I wish you would get up enough gumption to step to me," Quincy said before he felt a hand on his shoulder.

"Be cool, Q. You're better than that. We didn't come here for this!" Will told him.

Quincy suddenly felt ashamed of his actions and of the fact that a warrior like Will had to speak peace into his life.

"Look, man, I don't know you, but I respect you for coming here," Will said to Dwight.

"Good looking, fam. I appreciate it." Dwight gave Will a fist bump.

"But on the real, you don't want it with Q, and you're outnumbered." Will cut Dwight with his eyes.

There was a moment of tension before everyone at the table erupted in laughter.

"But I'm saying, though. It's nothing. I would've taken my beat down like a man, because I ain't no punk," Dwight snapped at Will.

"I know you're not a punk, but my whole point is, don't be a punk to your child," Quincy said, once again assuming control of the conversation. "I find it amazing how guys won't run from a fight even though they are severely outnumbered, but they'll run from fatherhood and they'll leave their child outnumbered."

The men at the table went silent, as they were considering the strength of Quincy's words. Quincy could tell that his words had an effect on Dwight, because Dwight became withdrawn from the group and stared at an empty space on the table.

"Be there. That's all I got to say. Even if you and the baby moms ain't getting along, just be there and everything will be all right," Will added.

Quincy cringed at the term *baby momma* being applied to Sasha. She was not some näive teenage girl who couldn't keep her legs closed, but at the moment she was in the same boat.

"Listen, I raised my daughter to be independent, so she's not like these others." Quincy did the quotation marks gesture. "Baby mommas that are on WIC, welfare, child support, you name it. She's going to be okay. Regardless, I will make sure of that."

"But not every girl has a father that's well off like you, Q. They need that support," Jamal said.

"The way I see it, there's no need for the baby's father to be present in the child's life if he's going to be a negative role model. That's all I'm saying." Quincy leaned back and hoped that Dwight could read between the lines.

"But that's not in the scriptures," Chauncey interjected.

"Of course not. It's being practical. The Bible does not have a road map for baby daddies. Isn't it God's will for a man and woman to marry?" Quincy said.

"Of course, but just because it doesn't always happen that way does not mean that the Bible does not have an answer for any situation," Chauncey replied.

Quincy said, "But there's a practicality in the Bible that you always overlook, Deacon. Faith without work is—".

"Is dead," Will said as he observed his brother, who had just put on some headphones to listen to music.

"There you go. So the question that I have for this young brother right here is, do you have faith, and are you willing to work?" Quincy focused his attention on Dwight, who was clearly lost in the discussion.

"Yeah, man. I'm going to be on my grind, getting it in until the fam is set."

"I guess that means you're going to work hard. The only other thing I have to say, and then I'll leave it alone, is keep it legit," Quincy said before he leaned back to rest.

"So, Brother Jamal, how are things with you and Chantel?" Chauncey asked.

"Man, this premarital counseling is no joke. It got us thinking about things and talking about things that never crossed Chantel's and my mind."

"But it's going good, right?" Chauncey asked.

"We argue more now than we did before. I mean, we argue over stupid stuff, like whether or not to fry the chicken or bake the chicken."

Quincy laughed, much to his own amusement.

"That's what marriage is about. At first you're going to argue a lot, so it's good that you get started now."

"I've never heard anyone say arguing is good," Dwight said.

"It keeps you honest. It creates an environment where you're not pretending, but you're keeping it real. There's nothing wrong with arguing so long as there are ground rules," Quincy said before he took a sip of his tea.

"Ground rules?" Will asked.

"Yeah. You notice that before every fight the ref reminds the fighters of the ground rules so that it can be a good clean fight? Karen and I's ground rules are as follows. . . ." Quincy started to count on his hand. "Number one, we are not going to use the word *divorce*. Number two, we are not going to compare ourselves to anyone else's marriage, and number three, we are not going to throw anything, including lamps, china, cats, and especially fists."

The men at the table chuckled and nodded. Quincy hoped that Dwight was taking in the information.

"That's something that we should have, but a relationship is different when you live together," Jamal said.

"I know you and Sister Chantel are not living together," Chauncey interjected.

The room became incredibly dense and uncomfortable. Quincy knew about Jamal and Chantel living together. He had advised Jamal not to move in and had been willing to help Jamal with other arrangements, but Jamal had insisted that moving in was the best thing to do, and he had asked Quincy to keep this secret to himself and not share it with everyone, especially Chauncey.

"Brother Jamal!" Chauncey said.

"We lived together for a brief moment, until we talked with Pastor Brown and I decided to move out until after the wedding. I'm staying with Will," Jamal explained.

"Brother Will, you knew about this?" All Chauncey got from Will was a head nod. "How come you didn't tell me?" Chauncey's eyes bounced from Jamal to Will in search of an answer.

"The code," Will said.

"What code?" Chauncey asked, even more confused.

"The guy code," Jamal said.

"I'm not gay," Chauncey shouted, then realized he was talking too loudly and lowered his voice. "I'm not gay."

"No one is saying you're not a guy, genius. It's just that you walk around so high and mighty that no one wants to tell you anything," Quincy said.

"I tell you guys everything!" Chauncey huffed.

"Oh really? Then when were you going to tell us about your little dating adventures?" Jamal asked.

At this point, Will was beyond confused. "C, you got a girl?"

"No. It's just that it's not good for a man to be alone. I would like to have a helpmate, so I've tried dating," Chauncey said.

"You're not going to find her if you're being too judgmental," Jamal said.

"Brother Jamal, I just want you and Chantel to be covered and for God to bless your relationship. Forgive me for trying to hold you accountable," Chauncey said.

"Look, C, I appreciate everything you do, but sometimes I just need you to be my brother in Christ and pray with me. As opposed to constantly showing me where I missed it," Jamal said.

"I don't think I'm that bad," Chauncey replied, and a score of murmurs from the table followed.

"C, I know I messed up, but I'm trying to do what's right, and I just need you guys' support," Jamal said.

Chauncey did not respond to Jamal's statement. Quincy wondered what everyone thought about Chauncey dating. Chauncey had expressed his desire to find a wife, but Quincy just had not known until this point the lengths to which Chauncey had gone in order to accomplish this goal.

"Chauncey, what kind of woman are you looking to marry?" Quincy asked.

"Well, she has to be a saved woman," Chauncey replied.

"We know that," Quincy said.

"Well, I don't know. The rest is just complicated. Lately it just seems like every time I look up, someone is getting married. You start to wonder if you're going to die alone." Chauncey started to scratch the back of his neck, which, Quincy knew, was a sign that he was uncertain.

"You're not going to die alone, C. You got your brothers, and you will find a good wife that can put up with you," Jamal said.

"Lord, have mercy," Quincy said after a sip from his iced tea.

"You're a good dude, C. God's got a good woman waiting for you," Will said.

"I'm just wondering if I can be patient to wait on her," Chauncey replied.

"That's that forty-year-old virgin talking," Quincy said.

After a moment of awkward silence, everyone proceeded to laugh. Quincy knew that with all that was going on between the four of them, it was going to be an eventful weekend indeed.

# Chapter Seventeen

## *Chauncey*

"Lord, forgive me for being distracted."

Chauncey did not expect to begin his morning with a prayer of repentance. He did not go into a bar or solicit a prostitute, though the environment surrounding the retreat was a distraction. His prayer was more for his growing disdain for being a part of the single men's workshops year after year. He wanted a wife. His brother, Henry, was a clear example of how difficult it was to die alone, with no woman by one's side. Yes, he had his sister, but he had lived too much of his life without a companion. Chauncey was determined not to suffer the same fate as Henry.

He finished up his morning devotional and made his way to the conference room. It was embarrassing for a forty-six-year-old man not to be married. Chauncey arrived at the conference room first, for a workshop that was focused on being a single Christian man of integrity. In light of last year's fiasco with Minister Jacobs, Chauncey had grown skeptical about taking pointers from a single Christian man about being a single Christian man. He needed to be taught by someone who had survived being single.

Dwight entered the conference room and took a seat next to Chauncey. Chauncey was surprised to see that Dwight was up early and was on time, even though the only difference in his appearance from yesterday, when Chauncey first met him, was the fact that he now had on a white tank top instead of a gray one.

"Hey, Brother Dwight. How are you?" Chauncey asked.

"I'm okay. I've never been to one of these before," Dwight replied.

"Did your father or your grandmother ever take you to church?"

"Man, if my father was to walk in here right now and sit down, I wouldn't even recognize him. My grandmother used to have me in church all Sunday, and I mean all Sunday, from the crack of dawn until late at night. When I got old enough, I got as far away from church as possible."

Chauncey loved church. He lived for an opportunity to be in God's presence, but he knew that made him different from most men. He noticed that most young men, when they turned eighteen, would run far away from the church. He never knew what caused them to want to turn away from God. All he knew was that God had a hand in bringing them back to church.

"I've never been to one of these, though." Dwight cleared his throat. "So what are they going to do? Talk to us or something?"

Chauncey chuckled and patted Dwight on the back. "Yes, brother . . . I'm sorry, but you never told me your last name."

"Oh, I don't like for people to call me by my last name. Just call me Dwight or D."

"Okay, Brother Dwight. An awesome man of God will come in and talk to us, and you just have to open yourself up and let God speak to you."

"I don't know. I haven't talked to God in so long, I don't know what to say." Dwight hung his head in shame.

"Son, God has forgiven you. The question is, will you forgive yourself?"

Will entered the conference room in his signature black T-shirt and jeans. Will had a seat next to Chauncey. Chauncey took a moment to examine his open collared shirt and slacks and wondered if he was overdressed for the occasion.

"Brother Will, how are you?" Chauncey said.

"Good. Just tired," Will replied.

"Same here, but Mr. Page told me I have to come here," Dwight said.

"Yeah, man, but it's cool to come and learn about walking right as a single Christian," Will answered.

"Chauncey, how come you're still single?" Dwight asked.

At first Chauncey was put off by Dwight's question. Chauncey did not want to engage in a discussion about his social life with Dwight.

"Well, I haven't met the woman that God would want me marry, that's all." Chauncey let out a nervous laughter.

Dwight shook his head. "Man, I don't know. A man your age that ain't married sounds a little suspect to me."

Will leaned forward to make eye contact with Dwight, who was on the other side of Chauncey. "Hey, man, don't disrespect Chauncey. This man changed my life. If he's waiting for God to bless him with a wife, then I respect that."

Brother Cage, one of the last single ministers, approached the podium. "Praise the Lord, brothers. Before we get started, we need to pray. We can't do anything without prayer."

Chauncey followed Brother Cage's lead and bent his head down to pray. Even though Chauncey words were centered in prayer, his thoughts were on Will and Dwight. Chauncey did not know what to do with Will, who was a reformed thug, and Dwight, who was a practicing one. He leaned back in the chair just in case they came to blows.

"My bad, man," Dwight said to Chauncey.

"Well, Brother Will, I know you have a fan club when it comes to some of the ladies of the church," Chauncey said.

"To be real with you, C, I'm all about my walk. I'm not trying to get with a woman when my own life is not together."

Chauncey decided to pan around the room. He felt guilty for not paying attention to the workshop, but it was all a rerun to him. He looked around, and he stopped to examine a brother who looked familiar, but he could not put his figure on it.

"Will." Chauncey nudged Will. "Haven't we seen that brother from somewhere before?"

"Man, where did you learn how to whisper?" Will asked before he looked in the direction that Chauncey pointed. "That's ole boy who was messing around with Q's wife."

Will was right. The man was the disgraced minister Jacobs. He had grown a beard and had picked up at least twenty pounds. Minister Jacobs was a clear example of the penalty for not walking in integrity. Chauncey took note.

"I wonder why he's here," Chauncey said.

"Seriously, C, are you going to talk to me this whole time?" Will replied.

Chauncey did not want to hinder Will's progress and growth as a single man of God, but he could not help but to take frequent glances at Minister Jacobs and wonder what would happen when Quincy found out he was here.

# Chapter Eighteen

## *Jamal*

Jamal felt like he had snuck into a party, uninvited. There was not a single unfamiliar face in the room. He had broken bread with all of them and had referred to all of them as brother, but he was not their brother at this hour. He was an outcast, an emblem of freedom that some of them envied.

"Jamal, what are you doing here?" Brother Thomas asked.

"You know I'm about to be one of you, so Pastor Dawkins figured I needed to start coming to the married men sessions."

Brother Thomas did not give a look of approval. He instead scratched his head, perplexed by the whole ordeal. "Well, Pastor knows what's best. Just know that marriage isn't easy. Good luck!"

"Luck? Luck has nothing to do with marriage. I mean, am I right?" Jamal asked.

Brother Thomas only snickered, and he made his way toward a group of brothers that were already locked into a deep conversation. Moments later Pastor Dawkins entered the conference room with Pastor Alder of New Covenant Christian Center. Pastor Alder reminded Jamal of the gospel musician Israel. He was light-skinned, a little on the chubby side, had short black hair, and wore glasses.

"Let's give the Lord a great big hand clap," Pastor Alder said as he clapped.

Pastor Alder had visited Greater Anointing on several occasions, and it was customary that he would have a praise session before he began to speak. Once the men in the room started clapping and singing praise to God, Pastor Alder settled them down with his hands.

"Okay, it's time to feed our spirit man before we go and feed our carnal man. Amen." Pastor Alder waited for the brothers to respond with an "amen" before he continued. "Job thirty-one, verse one, says, 'I made a covenant with my eyes. Why then should I think on a maid?' Brothers, if we are going to be men of integrity, then we have to have this same mind-set. You cannot be a married man with a single man's eyes."

Chuckles erupted throughout the conference room. What Jamal appreciated the most about Pastor Alder was that he did not mince words. He said what he believed, and did not care who he made feel uncomfortable as a result.

The pastor went on. "I know that sister at your job is fine, but please believe the problems you are having with your wife today that are causing you to look elsewhere, you will have those same problems and worse with that sister if you choose to leave your wife. And I say worse because right now God has His blessing over your marriage and can turn things around in your life."

"But how is it possible for a man to not look at another woman? I mean, I'm a man, and I see everything from cleavage to thongs. How am I supposed to ignore that?" asked one brother, whom Jamal did not know.

"By yourself, you can't do anything, but with God all things are possible," Pastor Alder replied. "You have to allow God to show you how that seemingly harmless look can open the door for the devil to destroy your marriage."

Jamal allowed Pastor Alder's words to sink in. Jamal had to see the devil at work on trying to destroy a Christian family. It wouldn't be long before Jamal took his vows, and he knew that many of the men in the room wanted to shout from the rafters for him not to do it.

Jamal knew that Chantel was the right woman for him. He just did not know how his life would change after he said "I do." He listened to brother after brother as they purged themselves of mental and emotional frustration. He prayed that he would not suffer the same fate.

# Chapter Nineteen

## *Titus*

The Shepherds of the Round Table was inspired by the tale of King Arthur and his Knights of the Round Table. King Arthur's greatness lay in his ability to refrain from seeing himself as superior to his fellow man. The Shepherds of the Round Table was a group of local pastors who usually met quarterly to discuss different topics. It was an opportunity for the pastors to discuss whatever issues perplexed them the most, whether of a personal or a professional nature.

Titus had invited his fellow members of the prestigious group to this year's men's retreat. He had decided that it was best to have an impromptu meeting at lunch, a meeting that he would later regret.

"Yeah, Doc, you've been missing in action," said Pastor Clemons, who reminded Titus of a black Santa Claus.

"I tell you about brothers that get married and start to do disappearing acts," said Pastor Combs, a robust pastor who was the same age as Titus.

"Don't hate because I enjoy coming home to my wife," Titus replied.

"So do we, but we haven't forgotten that we have a church to run as well." Pastor Clemons's belly shook with laughter.

"That's true. I've had a lot of women join in the last year from Greater Anointing, citing that things are different," Pastor Cooper said.

If there was such thing as an heir apparent to Pastor Dawkins's legacy as an eligible bachelor of the cloth, then Pastor Cooper had taken up the mantle. Cooper was young, good-looking, and a great practitioner of the Word. The news that Pastor Cooper had taken on some of Titus's admirers provoked in Titus both a little bit of envy and a little bit of relief that the temptation of provocative women had been reduced.

"I hear you guys belly ache about your wives wanting you to spend more time at home and less time at the church. That's not the kind of marriage I want. I would feel like I've failed as a husband if that happened," Titus said.

"I understand where you're coming from, but you've got to remember that you have a great calling, and to be a shepherd to men and women is not a calling that you can punch a clock on," Pastor Clemons said.

The waitress arrived and brought each man his respective meal. For a few minutes, Titus chewed on both his chicken cacciatore and the conversation. Prior to the meeting, Titus had chalked up most of the grumblings from his members as simple envy or codependence on the head pastor. This was the first time Titus had entertained the notion that maybe he was neglecting his flock while enjoying the warmth and pleasures of marriage. Titus's pasta grew cold as he mulled over his plight.

Pastor Alder, who had just delivered a great workshop, motioned to speak.

"What's on your mind, Doc?" Titus asked before he took a sip of his tea.

"I know you're having troubles with the sisters of your church, but just think about how difficult this has been for Grace. She married the elusive, enigmatic Pastor Dawkins, and most of the women in the church are wondering what's so special about her."

"I can't begin to describe what it's like to be with a woman that can make you feel both vulnerable and secure at the same time. Everything has changed as a result of being with Grace, and I know that things cannot go back to the way they were before I got married," Titus explained. "I'm not sure if I would want things to change if they could. I'm having trouble trying to figure out how to balance ministry and marriage."

"Um, well, she understands it, because she married you knowing who you are, but you've got to keep your priorities in order, because according to the Word, your wife comes first. Now, you also have a successful ministry, so you have to balance that too," Pastor Alder said.

Titus nodded. "I know, and I've been praying that God will help me to find that balance. I've done a pretty good job of fighting off the demons of my past. I come from a line of preachers who were womanizers. One would say it's in my blood, but I have fought and prayed hard for the Lord to deliver me from that lifestyle."

"You better be careful. A couple of years of marriage and you won't resemble the good-looking Pastor Dawkins. Your stomach will resemble a tire from Pep Boys. Then that's when the devil will send your Delilah. A fine, pretty little thing that will make you feel young again. That's when you, my friend, will find yourself in an intense test," Pastor Combs said.

Pastor Combs's words really resonated with Titus. Combs had been a leader of a ten-thousand-member congregation that seemed both unstoppable and invincible. Whenever he asked for his congregation to give, they would do it faithfully, and there was no building or project that they could not complete. Then his Delilah appeared, and the affair brought his ministry crashing down like a house of cards. Titus both revered and admired Combs, who was a passionate expositor of the Word.

"How have you been, Pastor Combs?" Titus asked.

"Well, my divorce was finalized this week. Twenty-six years." Pastor Combs put his head down and tried to eat. Some of the other brothers put their hands on his shoulders for comfort.

"Don't worry, Pastor. This too shall pass, and God will restore both you and your family," Titus said.

Titus's words were met with sobs from Pastor Combs. His heart ached for his fallen brother, and he prayed that God would restore Combs to the place he belonged. Titus also prayed that he would avoid the same mistakes that Pastor Combs had made.

# Chapter Twenty

## *Quincy*

Quincy needed to show Dwight that he was the man. At least that was what he told himself. In truth, Quincy was searching for some piece of control and power in an otherwise powerless situation. The boys skipped a heavy meal in exchange for fruit smoothies and a trip to the gym. Quincy added 305 pounds of weight to the weight-lifting bar, an amount that he had not lifted since college. Quincy, however, did not lack in the area of confidence. He pressed the weight-lifting bar up off the safety catch bars and felt its full gravity as it free-fell, until Dwight grabbed it just before it reached Quincy's throat. The results could have been either fatal or paralyzing.

Dwight possessed enough strength to return the bar back to its original position. "You all right?" he asked.

Quincy nodded. "Yeah, I'm good. It just slipped a little."

Dwight went back to lifting dumbbells as Jamal entered the gym and made his way over to the dumbbell rack and began lifting. Quincy got up and walked over to the dumbbell rack and stood next to Jamal. He grabbed two dumbbells, and both men stared at each other in the reflection of the mirror.

"You know, Q, eventually you're going to have to give the boy a chance. He came here, and that says something."

"What he does when he becomes a father will tell me all that I need to know." Quincy winced from the weight of the dumbbells.

"I know you don't want to accept the fact that Sasha is not the only one that's going to need you. Dwight is going to need you too." Jamal set the weights down and wiggled his arms as he loosened up.

"What happened to this generation?" Quincy set down the dumbbells and put his hands on his hips. He seemed to have asked the question in a rhetorical sense. "My great-grandfather passed down the building blocks of success. Educated and the Bible. More than half of the members of my family have college degrees and are successful entrepreneurs. Where did we mess up? What did we do to cause kids not to value a better way of life, as opposed to struggling?"

"Nothing. The scriptures says that life and chance happen to us all. The rain falls on the just and unjust. You've raised Sasha right, and I know she'll find her way back to what you and Karen taught her." Jamal picked up the weights and started lifting again. "My grandmother instilled the Bible in me and the importance of making Jesus my Lord and Savior. When everything in the world failed, God was there to take me back in. God has not left Sasha, and you'll be amazed at how she will turn around."

"We'll see," Quincy said. Jamal's words did find a place in Quincy's psyche. If anyone could rebound from a setback, it was Sasha. She carried the same resolve as Quincy.

Quincy and Jamal both took a break from working out to grab water bottles from a nearby vending machine. They took sips from their water bottles and watched Chauncey attempt to run on the treadmill before he ended up getting a cramp.

"Oh, help me, Jesus," Chauncey said as he grabbed his leg.

Quincy could not hold back the laughter, and neither could Jamal and Dwight. For once they were all in accord.

"God don't like ugly." Chauncey winced as he took a seat on one of the benches.

"Well, how He explain you?" Quincy asked.

"Oh, Brother Page, I pray for you. I pray that the Lord is merciful and does not curse you for talking about His anointed," Chauncey said.

Quincy wondered if a curse was the best explanation of his situation. Quincy's business had thrived while other businesses had collapsed. How come he could not transfer that success from his company to his home?

# Chapter Twenty-one

## *Dwight*

"You have been here long enough. Do you under-stand me?" Pastor Snow said. "You have been here long enough, and it is time to break up your fallow ground and march into your destiny."

Dwight had never heard someone as powerful as Pas-tor Snow. He had heard Bob Marley sing, Tupac rap, and Farrakhan speak, but no one had ever captivated him like Pastor Snow did. Chill bumps broke loose all over his skin. They gave his tattoos an eerier 3-D effect. He needed to regain control of his faculties.

"Let me tell you why you've been going around in circles." Pastor Snow paused to wipe the sweat from his forehead. "It's because you've been living for yourself. No one achieves greatness living for themselves. God created you for a purpose, and if you're not here to fulfill that purpose, then you're going to continue to live for yourself. You were called to impact a nation and a gen-eration."

Dwight had never seen himself as a great man. He didn't even think he had the potential to do anything great, other than make music. Even his aspirations with music had selfish motives. But as he sat in the chair, he felt his heart starting to enlarge. He felt his heart being filled with a capacity to want to do more.

He had been unsure about a lot of things, especially with Sasha's father being upset over his baby girl being pregnant, but as he sat and listened to the scripture, nothing else mattered.

"Don't wait," urged Pastor Snow. "If you're man enough and bad enough to put the foolish things behind you, then persist and put the foolishness behind you. I want you to head down to this altar right here, and we are going to pray and give our lives to God. Don't surrender to the circumstance. Surrender to God."

Surrender. He had always view the word *surrender* as a synonym for *weakness,* but the way Pastor Snow spoke with such conviction, *surrender* did not seem like a negative word. Pastor Snow made eye contact with each man, and though he stood only five foot, four inches, his intensity was that of an all-pro lineman.

"When Elisha was working on his parents' farm and had an encounter with the prophet Elijah, he dropped everything, because at that moment he knew he had met his destiny and purpose. What will you do when you encounter your destiny? What will you give up to become the man God has created you to be?"

Dwight felt the desire that had started within his heart turn into a fire that ignited and spread throughout the core of his being. He had goose bumps that did not go away. Tears welled up in his eyes. Dwight was having a nervous breakdown, but it felt so good that he did not care. He wanted a destiny; he wanted a purpose. He wanted to be like the prophet in the Bible, to meet his destiny and not give it a second thought.

"Don't wait," said Pastor Snow. "Come down here right now, and let's get on the path to becoming what God has always intended for you to be."

Men started to fill the altar. Dwight's skin was still riddled with goose bumps. He felt two distinct hands touch each of his shoulders. He looked to his left, and there was Will. Dwight turned to his right, and there was Jamal. Both had a smile on their face.

"If you want to go, we'll go with you," Jamal said.

Dwight could give only a head nod, and his feet felt heavy, but as long as Will and Jamal had their hands on his shoulders, he felt like he could make it. His knees buckled as he got closer to the altar and saw men already on the floor, praying. He arrived and locked eyes with Pastor Snow.

"Young man, do you surrender to God?" Pastor Snow put the microphone to Dwight's lips.

*Surrender to God, not to circumstances.* That sounded like a powerful way to live, and Dwight was tired of running around, chasing the pipe dream of being a producer.

"I surrender to God, and I want to be what God wants me to be." Dwight collapsed to his knees under the weight of the words. Will and Jamal took a knee with him as he prayed.

"Lord, I know I've done messed up, and I ain't got much to show for with my life. But I'm here, and I'm willing to do whatever it takes to be close to you and make you proud of me," Dwight prayed.

Dwight continued to pray until he could no longer kneel, and when that happened, he lay face down on the floor and prayed some more, until the conference room carpet was stained with his sweat and tears. He thought about his mother's, who loved him and had done the best she could for him, and how he had rejected her love for the sake of being cool. He thought about all those times he could've died at the wrong place and the wrong time. Nothing he had done up until this point was worthy of grace and forgiveness. Dwight did not feel worthy of a second chance, but he had one. He prayed through the pain, and it seemed like the more sweat and tears poured out, the more release he felt from his past.

He felt weak and powerful at the same time, but Dwight had been reborn without reentering the womb. Dwight felt like shouting. It was as if he had been born for the first time, and he knew that his life would never be the same.

# Chapter Twenty-two

## *Titus*

Titus was in the middle of a card game with his staff when a knock on the door alerted him that he had an impromptu visitor. One of Titus's armor bearers got up.

"I got it." Titus motioned for his armor bearer to sit down. Titus made it to the door after a second set of knocks. He opened the door and saw Will on the other side.

"Pastor, I know you're busy, but I really need to talk with you," Will said.

"Sure." Titus gave Will a head nod and stepped aside and let him enter the hotel room.

*Need* was not a word that Titus was accustomed to hearing from Will. Titus dismissed his staff and took a seat at the table, where Will already sat.

"So what's going on, Will?"

"Man, I just don't know what to do with my family. I feel like giving up and turning them over to God."

"Well, I agree with turning them over to God, but I'm not sure about giving up on your family."

"What am I supposed to do? I try real hard to help them, but at what cost? I'm literally risking my life just to see them, and they don't want to get right."

For someone as young as Will to possess so much passion for his family was impressive. Titus had discovered a long time ago that he lived in an age where children grew more and more indifferent. Respect for family had dissipated, and respect for elders was non-existent.

"I mean, my family takes me places where I'm not trying to go," Will added.

"What do you mean?" Titus asked.

"I mean, I used to be a real hot-head. I blamed my family, because love seemed to dwell everywhere else but in our home. So I used to walk around with this mentality that if you said something to me, then that was it. We were throwing them." Will started to shadowbox. "Ever since I gave my life over to God, I feel like I got this anger boiling over and at any minute I can lose it."

"That means that there are aspects of your life that you have not given over to God. Listen to me." Titus tapped Will on the knee to get his attention. "Every sin, every failure, every imperfection or misplaced emotion, every inadequate feeling you have, Christ placed those on the cross with Him and they died with Him. You don't have to feel like you're going to lose it, because what you have gained is far greater."

Will put his head down, and Titus was not sure if it was because of the weight of his problems or shame about his feelings. Titus gave him time to think and meditate on what he had said.

"How do I let go of what my family did to me? I want to love them. I want to be a family, but I don't know what to do," Will said as he lifted his head up.

"You, of all people, should know. Wasn't it you who held one of my most dedicated members at gunpoint and forced him to bring you to last year's retreat? Weren't you the same person who turned his life around and gave his life over to God?"

"Yeah," Will said with a smirk.

"The same God who brought you out of darkness into light is just as capable of doing the same thing with your family. You just have to be an instrument of peace, love and, above all, forgiveness. God will work it out."

"Thank you so much, Pastor." Will stood up and extended his hand.

"I'm very proud of you," Titus said as he shook Will's hand. "Listen, I needed to step out for a minute to take care of a few things before the next service."

"No problem," Will said as he headed toward the door.

Titus followed Will out the door and made his way toward the lobby. He was excited about the breakthrough he had just had with Will. Titus felt motivated for tonight's service. He entered the lobby with Will, and everything went into slow motion. His eyes focused on a strikingly tall figure. *It can't be.*

"Will, I'm going to have to catch up with you later. I'll come by after today's service for my haircut." Titus patted Will on his back without taking his eyes off the figure in the distance.

"Okay, Pastor, no doubt." Will reversed course and headed back toward his hotel room, while Titus walked forward.

The closer he got to the figure, the less obscure it became. He still had a head full of hair, though it was more salt than pepper. Titus was jealous that a man twenty-two years his senior had more hair than he did. When Titus had closed in him and was just twenty feet away, a smile crept over the man's face. There was nothing for Titus to smile about. Titus stopped three feet from the man, which was close enough for him to have a conversation with him or grab him by the throat.

"Good to see you, son," Lemont Dawkins said to his only child.

Titus heard "Son," and he was fifteen again. Lemont's voice was full of approval, which was what Titus had longed for over the years. The warmth and love for his father that filled Titus lasted a moment.

"You obviously are here for a reason, so . . ." Titus gestured for his father to explain his reason for being at the retreat.

"I don't know where to start." Lemont took a step toward Titus.

"Why you're here would be a good start," Titus said.

"I missed you, and I wanted to see you. It took me this long to get up the courage to come see you."

"It only took you thirty years. Well, here I am." Titus threw up his hands. "Now, if you would excuse me, I have a sermon to deliver." Titus turned to walk away.

"Wait!" Lemont stretched out his hand and touched Titus on the shoulder. Titus felt anger rise up within him, and he threw his father's hand off with his shoulder.

"Titus, I wanted to say that I'm proud of you."

"I know that," Titus replied.

"And I'm sorry." Lemont's voice cracked, and tears started to leak from his eyes.

"I know. I can hear it in your voice and see it in your eyes," Titus said as he turned around and faced his father. "If you're here to tell me you're sorry or that you want me to forgive you, then save it. I know that you're sorry, and I forgave you a long time ago. I just want to know what you hoped to accomplish by showing up here."

"I was hoping that you can find it in your heart to let me be your father again. I don't want to go the rest of my life without a relationship with my son."

"You've got to be kidding me! I'm forty-five years old. What are you going to father me through? My golden years? You weren't there when I blew my knee out in college. You weren't there when I graduated college. Where were you when I preached my first sermon? Where were you when I got married? The events that shaped me, you were absent from, so I don't see why you need to be in my life now."

"What I'm asking for is a lot, but I just don't want you to go the rest of your life hating me."

Titus looked into his father's eyes and saw a stranger. Gone was the superhuman pedestal that Titus had once put his father on. Titus saw before him a man that was broken and scared.

"For years I asked myself, why did you hate Mom and me? Titus took a step back and covered his mouth to hide the empathy in his voice. "After all these years of seeing how you leaving affected my mother and me, I realized that I was asking the wrong questions. The real question I should've been asking was, why do you hate yourself?"

Titus could tell his father was puzzled by his question.

"You must not love yourself if you could walk away from a family that loves you. I bet you're not even with the woman who you left us for," Titus added.

Lemont nodded his head in agreement. Titus figured the shame for his actions prevented him from speaking.

"I bet it's a lot easier to walk away from a mistress after you've walked away from your family. I think you're here because after all these years of walking away from your calling and everything that matters, you realized that the problem was never us or the calling. It was within you."

"You don't understand that there are things within our family that go back farther than you know."

"You're talking about the curse. Every day I look in the mirror and I face the demons of my past, and every day, by the grace of God, I put those things under my feet. There ain't no curse that is more powerful than Jesus. The devil is a liar."

Titus's eyes betrayed him, and so did his father's. Tears streamed down his face, and Titus did not bother to wipe them, because he was a man and he was not afraid of his emotions.

"Listen, Dad, I have to go do what God has called me to do, and I think that what is more important than any other relationship you have is the one you have with God, and God is waiting for you to return to Him. You don't owe me anything. I survived, and Momma survived. You owe it to yourself to get right." Titus turned and walked away.

"Titus," Lemont said to Titus's back.

Titus did not break his stride. He knew what he did was not right, but it was time for his father to call out to him. And it was time for Titus not to respond to his father's pleas.

Titus walked back to his room and felt a little disappointed with himself. True, he had stood up to his father and had said the things he needed to say, but he had weakened his stance by being vengeful. Titus could've responded to his father's plea for him to come back. Forgiveness was the name of the game, and Titus had lost that round.

# Chapter Twenty-three

## *Quincy*

Last year at the circle of power, Quincy discovered who the man was that had had an affair with his wife, and proceeded to throw a chair and act a fool. This year he wanted to lay low and fly below the radar. He sat alone in a chair in an elongated conference room. It was clear that this room could be used as two rooms, because it had the divider toward the middle. The divider had been pulled back so that the circle would be big enough for the men at the conference. With his arms folded, he thought about how God had laid a difficult path for him to walk. First, through an affair, now through an unexpected pregnancy. Quincy wondered if he would have the courage to voice his concern and seek counsel from his brothers. He had to admit that Dwight was not the hopeless case that he originally thought he was. Dwight, like a lot of young men, needed guidance.

"Hey, Brother Page. Did you get the memo?" Brother Hawkins asked.

"What memo?"

"That whatever chair you sit in, it has to be screwed down." Brother Hawkins started to laugh, and he put his fist out for Quincy to give him a pound. Of course, Quincy left him hanging.

Quincy did not mind being teased. He had thick skin, and he could give as good as he got, but he refused to let someone who was not a close friend tease him, which was the case with Brother Hawkins.

"Q!"

Quincy turned around to see who had called his name with such urgency. He saw that Jamal, Will, Chauncey, and Dwight were entering the conference room. They seemed concerned, which made Quincy nervous.

"What's up?"

"Listen, man, don't trip, but there's something I have to tell you," Jamal said as he stopped right in front of Quincy. Quincy was even more concerned now because the other guys seemed to form a half circle, which blocked his view of the door.

"What's wrong?" Quincy asked.

Before Jamal could respond, Quincy glanced over to his left, at the door. A man entered the conference room, and Quincy felt that urge to throw a chair when he realized it was Minister Jacobs. He looked god-awful.

"You've got to be kidding me. What is he doing here?" Quincy said.

"He needs this just as much as we do," Jamal replied.

Minister Jacobs gave a friendly, but timid wave, to which Quincy did not bother to respond. He had forgiven Minister Jacobs, which was huge for a guy like Quincy, who tended to be a little vindictive. But for Minister Jacobs to show up at the same event where he fell from grace was not only poor timing, but it was also bad form.

"You cool, Q?" Jamal asked.

"Yeah, I'm cool. Trust me, if I wasn't, you would know."

The circle of power started, and Quincy did not even pay attention to the testimonies he heard. He looked at Jacobs and wondered why he was there.

"Well, we got time for one more testimony," Pastor Dawkins said.

Minister Jacobs got up and made his way to the center of the circle. Quincy heard the murmurs and wondered what he was going to say.

"Brothers, I know it's been a minute, and I debated about coming here, but in the past year God has worked some things out in me." Minister Jacobs started to choke on his own words, and Quincy started to roll his eyes."For the last year I've been with family in Houston, and I've been studying God's word and trying to figure out where I went wrong. I have come because I wanted to apologize to Quincy Page."

Men started to turn and look at Quincy. Quincy wondered what Minister Jacobs's angle was.

"Minister Jacobs, you already apologized and I forgave you, remember?" Quincy said.

"Derrick. My name is Derrick Jacobs, and over the past year I discovered that I was not called to preach."

Whispers could be heard throughout the room, and Quincy was caught off guard by Jacobs's words.

"When I apologized to you last year, it was not sincere. It was all about me trying to save face so that one day I could be able to minister again and keep my position. But my desire to be a minister and be of importance in the church was not the result of a calling, but of a need to feel empowered." Jacobs walked toward Quincy, unafraid of what Quincy's reaction might be. He knelt down before Quincy as if Quincy were royalty and he was not worthy to stand before him.

"Please, Brother Quincy, forgive me for betraying you and for the pain I caused. I know God has forgiven me, but my mistake will stay with me for the rest of my life."

A man traveled from Houston to ask for forgiveness for something that he did a year ago. Quincy was in awe of the humility that Minister Jacobs had shown, and realized that he could not harbor any resentment for him. Quincy felt shame over his actions toward Dwight.

"Man, I forgive you." Quincy stood up, and what he did next was a shock to him. Quincy embraced Minister Jacobs in a hug, and both men shared a tear. Quincy understood at that moment why mercy was so important: because in the end he needed God's mercy.

# Chapter Twenty-four

## *Titus*

"Psalms twenty-two, one . . . 'My God, My God, why have you forsaken me!' Matthew twenty-seven, verse forty-six . . . 'My God, My God why have you forsaken me?'" Pastor Dawkins stepped away from the podium with his iPad in hand and walked in front of a packed conference room, which had also been the site of the circle of power about an hour ago. His mind was still stuck on seeing his father after thirty years. Titus looked at his message on his iPad and saw a sermon that he had connected with mentally but not spiritually. Deep within his heart and his spirit he knew there was something else he wanted to say. That sermon had remained aloof from Titus until his father entered the conference room and took a seat in the back.

"Forgiveness . . . ," Titus said to his surprise before he handed his iPad to one of his armor bearers sitting in the front row. "I had a sermon prepared to rally the troops and get you guys stirred up, but I must yield to the Holy Spirit, which is telling me to talk to you tonight about forgiveness." Titus paused to make sure he had everyone's attention. "There's nothing more toxic that can exist within a human being than unforgiveness. There is nothing it profits, and it does not even make the person that you're mad at suffer."

Words and ideas came at Titus like a tidal wave, and he paused for a moment to calm the waves and smoothly convey God's message. "If I was to peer into your lives, I would see points where you were rejected by someone who was supposed to love you. Some of you had teachers, neighbors, and church members who spoke words of unworthiness into your life, and as a result, you built up walls. You allowed all your emotions to erode, with the exception of anger. Anger has grown, and it has spawned bitterness."

Titus received a sprinkle of "Amens" throughout the room. This was not a sermon that was meant to elicit shouts. This sermon was meant to perform surgery. It was meant to cut through the flab and get to the heart of the matter.

He went on. "You cannot draw strength from anger. You can't find comfort in unforgiveness, because true power comes from being able to look both the offender and the offense in the eye and not trip."

The "Amens" grew louder, and a few men even stood up and pointed at Titus. Titus noticed that his father had stood up.

"How you know you're walking in power is when you don't react when someone mistreats you. You just keep doing what God called you to do. I have a purpose, and I'm going to fulfill it whether you're in my life or not. If you're trying to pull me down, then that means you're already beneath me, and instead going down to your level, I'm going to pull you up to mine."

Most of the men were out of their seats now, and the fire that had ignited within Titus's spirit was strong and vibrant.

"We have to become men after God's own heart. Make no mistake about it. In this life we will endure hardships, and you probably feel like God has forsaken you." Titus started to pace back and forth along the front row. "You've lost your job, your house, and your marriage ended in a bitter divorce. All of these things are worthy reasons to feel like God has left you. You lost a child, and you're still grieving over the loss. But in all that you go through, if you don't give up, God will cause you to triumph. Let it go. Let go of the pain, and accept forgiveness."

Men started to clap, and Titus got that feeling again. He likened that feeling to the taste of honey on wheat bread. It was sweet and healthy.

"If God can cause a shepherd that was ostracized and cast out of his own house to become a great king, then what is going on in your life that you can't over-come?" Titus did not expect an answer to his rhetorical question. He just wanted the brothers to think. "If God brought back Jesus from the grave, then what obstacle is in your way that you can't come back from?"

Now the men were on their feet, praising God and clapping and encouraging Titus to go on.

"When God created Adam and Eve, He gave them dominion, and they gave their dominion to Satan. When Jesus died on the cross and nailed your sins and my sins on the cross, He gave us back our dominion. You are meant to excel wherever you go. Don't give anyone power over you when God has given you the power to be more than a conqueror."

Men started to cry and fall on the floor in praise. Titus even got teary-eyed when he thought about the goodness of God.

"When Jesus was on the cross, he said to God, 'For-give them, for they know not what they do.' Forgive your teachers, for they didn't know who you were des-tined to become. Forgive your haters, because their ha-tred only strengthens you to become more like God and less like them." Titus paused and looked at his father. Lemont's eyes were full of tears. "And forgive your parents, because regardless if they were in your life or not, your Heavenly Father has never left you."

Titus summoned his deacons and ministers to come forth. Clyde, one of the musicians, assumed his position at the keyboard in the far right corner of the room and began to play a slow melody. Men started to walk from their seats to the altar for prayer.

Lemont made his way toward the front, and without a thought, Titus moved toward his father. They met in the middle of the room like two combatants about to do battle. Lemont did not say anything. He just extended his hands out for prayer.

"Pray for me," Lemont said.

Titus nodded his head, and for the first time since Titus was a teenager, he and his father prayed together.

# Chapter Twenty-five

## *Will*

Will and Joshua came back to the hotel room on fire from the Word they had just received, and even more on fire that Joshua had decided to give his life to the Lord.

"Man, I can't believe this. That service was active," Joshua said as he paced the floor. "Is this what you feel?"

"Yeah, bro. That's why I can't go back to the life I had."

"So what do we do now?" Joshua asked.

It was a legitimate question Joshua had asked. What was a free man supposed to do?

"We go and get our family back, and we do it together," Will answered.

"I'm scared," Joshua said as he sat and slumped on the bed.

"There's nothing to be afraid of. We're going to find a way to get you out of that life, and we're going to find a way to help our parents and little sister."

Joshua did not have a reply. He just dropped his head, conceding the point.

"Talk to me, Josh."

"It's like you're a changed person. You're not the brother I knew."

"Is that a good thing or a bad thing?"

"I don't know. It's just different. I know you love me and care for me, but I can't get with this. I don't know what happened."

"What happened is I stopped following the devil's plan and started following God's plan. I'm not trying to force my beliefs on you, Josh, but I am trying to get you to see that the path you're on now leads to destruction. You can have more nights like tonight."

Something else was wrong. The way Joshua's shoulder sank in, it was like he was spooked about something.

"What's wrong, Josh?"

"Last night I had a dream."

"Okay. What about?"

"It was me, Uncle Tony, and Dad, and we were in this bad Camaro like the one in *Transformers,* all black and silver. So we were driving, right, and it seems like we're in a desert or something, because it's just open land as far as we can see, and we're driving as fast as we can without a care in the world. Then, all of a sudden . . ." Joshua's words drifted off, and Will could tell that his brother was transfixed on the vivid details of his dream.

"What happened?" Will asked.

"There was no more road. It was like a cliff came out of nowhere, and we were too busy having a good time to notice that we had gone off the cliff until it was too late."

Joshua shook, as if a cold chill had come over him. Will did not consider himself a prophet. He was a simple man, but he understood exactly what that dream meant. A year ago he would have been a passenger in the ill-fated car. At times Will wondered if he was still on the edge or if he had escaped his fate.

"Josh, God don't make mistakes. Though there are some things beyond our understanding, other things are not. I believe God allowed you to see the road that you guys are headed down. You may feel like you got all this time in the world to mess up and then fix it later, but you don't. All things come to an end."

"Bro, I messed up so bad that there's no way I could be saved." Joshua started to cry.

"No one that is alive is beyond saving. You and I both draw breath, and we both can change."

"I know God has forgiven me, but what about the Untouchables? They're going to kill me when they find out." Joshua wiped his face with his midnight-blue T-shirt.

Will was heartbroken at the sight of his brother. The thought of Joshua being killed sent a chill through Will's body. "Joshua, who says that your life is over? If God is able to deliver me, then he's more than able to deliver and protect you. Do you understand?"

Joshua took an extra minute to wipe his face before he gave Will a head nod.

Will did not know if Joshua's silence was a result of what he had said to him or if Joshua was still thinking about the dream. One thing that Will knew for certain was that Joshua had experienced his own personal retreat.

# Chapter Twenty-six

## *Titus*

Titus found himself outside Jamal's door without an armor bearer. It was just him with his Air Jordan sweat suit on. He knocked on the door, and when Jamal answered, to Titus's surprise, he saw that the room was full. Will was in the midst of cutting hair, while Chauncey was reading his Bible. Quincy was looking through a magazine. Dwight, who, Titus knew, was the new young man who had accompanied Quincy to the retreat, lay on the bed, watching sports.

"What's good, Pastor?" Will said after he paused from cutting hair.

"Hey, now, I was coming to get my hair shaped up," Titus replied.

"I got you," Will said as he proceeded to cut Jamal's hair.

"Hey, Pastor!" Chauncey jumped up and made a beeline to Titus. Chauncey was a little uncomfortable to be around whenever he was overzealous. He shook Titus's hand and gave him a Christian hug. "I'm so glad to see you. I was just about to lead the brothers in devotion."

"Sure you were," Quincy said while he flipped through the magazine.

"Well, these brothers have had a long day, and that Word tonight will make anybody full," Titus said. "I think it is important for everyone to relax. So what's been up?"

"Nothing. Just chilling," Jamal said.

"How about you, Pastor? How are you enjoying married life?" Quincy asked.

"If I had known then what I know now." Titus laughed as he and Quincy exchanged fist bumps. "It's been good, but it's difficult. The sisters of the church are giving me a hard time."

"What do you expect? One of the most eligible bachelors in all of Southern California is married, and to an outsider, of all things. You know that's a tough pill to swallow." Quincy said.

"I was surprised that you got married, Pastor Dawkins," Chauncey said.

"Well, I was the type that was comfortable with just being alone and focusing on the gospel. It wasn't until Grace came into my life that I realized that something was missing," Titus explained.

"Hold on. You mean to tell me, Pastor, that you ain't never . . ." Dwight, whom Titus did not know, made gestures to substitute for what he really wanted to ask him. Titus knew he wanted to know about his sex life but did not have a way to ask that would not be considered inappropriate. Titus decided to let the young man off the hook.

"Well, I haven't always been a pastor. I have had my youthful indiscretions, which is why when God spoke to me in a motel room, of all places, after I had just gotten high and had sex, I thought He was tripping. I did not want to be a hypocrite, so I told God that he would have to help, and you know what?" Titus waited until he had the attention of everyone in the room. "He did!"

"Praise God," Jamal and Chauncey said in unison.

"So I see you guys are relaxing, so, Brother Will, if you wanted me to come back later for my haircut, I will," Titus said.

"Oh no. I'll fade you up real quick," Will replied.

"Yeah, Pastor, stay! We were just about to break out some cards," Quincy replied.

"Well, I don't want to have to administer a beat down at a men's retreat," Titus said as he chuckled to himself.

The other men in the room looked at each other with devilish grins.

Two hours later not only had Titus gotten his haircut, but he was still in Jamal's hotel room, enjoying a card game.

"Now, Pastor, I hope you don't take this whipping personally. I don't want to go home to a plague or locusts or anything like that," Quincy said.

"You're doing a whole lot of talking for someone who didn't make his books last hand," Titus replied.

"You talk a good one," Quincy said before he turned to Dwight. "You're a pretty good card player. Too bad."

"Brother Page, I'm not going to even pretend that I understand what you're going through, because I am not a father, but I do know this. If Dwight made the commitment to come here, then that's something," Titus said.

"You know, Pastor, with all due respect, I get tired of you always asking me to turn the other cheek," Quincy replied.

"It's because you're better than what your knee-jerk emotions are telling you. You are a great man, and I just want you not to allow your circumstances to cause you to think that you are anything less than that!" Titus pounded his fist on the table like a gavel.

"But that contradicts who I am. I am who I am today because I didn't bow down to anyone, and I'm not about to start doing that now. I'm sorry, Pastor, but I'm not that guy." Quincy threw his hands up in surrender.

"But you are a new creature with God. He had a plan for success, and His plan never fails. Remember, you are the righteousness of God. Don't become bitter because others become bitter toward you. Don't hang your head down because of someone else's actions, either." Titus noticed that the cards had stopped being dealt, and the side conversations had ceased as well. Titus had the full attention of his brothers, and the moment could not go to waste. "We have to stop blaming this generation for the mistakes they've made, and we must take ownership of it. Christians, we should be the first in line to offer compassion."

Titus turned to Dwight. "You have some critical decisions to make in the coming months, before this baby arrives. You have a great resource in Brother Quincy, and you have decided to give your life over to the Lord, which means that you have the recipe to be a successful father. Do you understand me?" Titus asked.

"Yeah." Dwight gave a nod. "I'm going to be a great father. I believe that now."

"The games stop now. You played, and now it's time to be a great example of a man for your child," Titus added.

"But, Pastor Dawkins, I would say that Jesus should be his greatest example," Chauncey said.

"Deacon, we are a reflection of Jesus, and if our children see a form of Jesus that drinks, that's abusive and mean, then our children will not want to have anything to do with the real Jesus!"

"That's true," Jamal said.

"We have to remember that we were all created to fulfill a purpose, and each of us has the capacity to accomplish much. But the choice comes down to what image you identify with—the one that has been shaped by the opinions and views of our families and community or the one that is a reflection of who God says you are in the Bible."

"That's a good word right there. We miss hearing that from you," Jamal said.

"I don't understand," Titus said.

"I mean, don't get me wrong, Pastor, and I respect your and Grace's marriage, but you have something that not every preacher has, and that is a finger on the pulse of men. Men come to Greater Anointing because they know that they are going to receive a Word that will help them deal with the circumstances of life," Jamal replied.

Titus had heard this statement from his detractors, fellow pastors, and now from the men of his congregation. There was something about the way Jamal presented his concern that made it finally hit home for Titus. Jamal did not want anything from him other than to hear a Word that would help him to be a better husband and a better father.

"Listen, brothers, I'm sorry if I've been a little MIA as a result of marital bliss." Titus's statement garnered a chuckle from Quincy. "Listen, I come from a long line of preachers who stepped out on their wives, and I can cite a host of other examples of pastors who can't keep their marriages together but can preach. That man you saw me hug and pray for tonight was my father, and that was the first time I've seen him in thirty years."

Shock swept through the room. Titus was neither an open book nor a sealed document. He told personal stories as he saw fit, and he'd kept his childhood guarded until now.

Titus went on. "I decided that if I was going to get married, then I was going keep everything in the proper perspective and put my wife first." Titus noticed how his thoughts were foreign to his brethren. "I would step away from the ministry to keep my marriage strong."

"The devil is a liar!" Chauncey said.

"It's not the devil. The devil has fooled us for so long into thinking that we have to be slaves to our professions in order to succeed. God has blessed me with a wife, and through her, I will become everything that God has wanted me to be," Titus said.

"That's heavy," Dwight said.

"I will be more mindful of my pastoral duties, because I do have a calling and I don't want you brothers to feel like you're not getting all you need," Titus admitted.

"Thanks, Pastor," Jamal said.

"Hey, Pastor, you know, I was thinking that maybe we should have an event like this," Will said as he shook some hair into a wastebasket.

"What do you mean, Will?" Titus asked.

"We should have an event kind of like a barbershop, but instead we talk about getting closer to God. I could see if I could get some of my friends from the college to volunteer."

"That would be a great way to minister to guys outside the church. I could find a venue," Quincy added.

"That sounds like a great idea," Titus said.

"You could probably advertise it on Facebook or Twitter," Jamal added.

"See, that's why you guys are my A-team, because you think outside the box, and that's what we're going to have to do to keep the church relevant," Titus replied.

"And that's what's important, Pastor. What has helped your ministry stand out is that you have been able to minister to men," Quincy said.

"You're right, Quincy. You're right!" Titus said, to which Quincy gave him a head nod.

And with Quincy words of wisdom, Titus knew what he had to do.

# Chapter Twenty-seven

## *Chauncey*

After the retreat, Chauncey went and visited the one person who understood him the best, his sister, Nicole. Since the death of his brother, Henry, he and Nicole had grown closer. But something had happened within just the last two months that had caused their closeness to be strained.

Chauncey arrived at the front door of his sister's house. After he rang the doorbell twice, the door was opened by Tory, a six-foot-one-inch headache. He was handsome, he had a good job, no kids, and he went to church. But in short, Chauncey did not think that he was right for his baby sister.

"C, man, what's good?" Tory asked.

"Deacon McClendon," Chauncey replied.

Tory gave Chauncey a little smirk and turned and called out, "Nikki!"

Nicole walked out of the kitchen with another woman by her side. They both wore a smile on their face. "Bighead, it's so good to see you."

Chauncey gave his baby sister a hug, and it felt good to feel the warmth of her embrace. He broke aware from Nicole's embrace to observe the fair-skinned beauty with captivating hazel eyes that stood next to her.

"Hello." The young woman extended her hand.

"Chauncey, this is my girlfriend, Rachel," Nicole announced.

"Hello, Rachel. It's a pleasure to meet you." Chauncey held Rachel's hand longer than he should have.

Chauncey realized that his invitation to dinner was an intricate plot set up by his sneaky sister. Nicole had made no mention of a fourth person, and a woman on top of that.

"Dinner is just about ready," Nicole told her brother. "Are you staying for dinner?"

"I think I will." Chauncey laughed inside at the absurdity of Nicole's question.

Chauncey was not inclined to spend an evening with Tory, to hear about his wonderful life as a business lawyer who coached baseball on the weekend, while feeding the homeless and attending every service on Sunday. He made Chauncey sick, but Chauncey couldn't deny his attraction to Rachel and his desire for his sister's above-average pot roast.

Chauncey followed Nicole into the dining room, where the sound of Mary J. Blige bounced off the walls. Chauncey felt his sister's choice in music was beyond inappropriate. For years Mary had been a symbol of depression and sexual promiscuity. Chauncey felt that by playing Mary J. Blige, his sister was inviting the spirit of promiscuity. Chauncey had a seat at the dining room table, which was decorated with an earth-toned tablecloth. Tory took a seat at the opposite end of the table, and Rachel sat next to Chauncey.

"So how was the men's retreat?" Nicole asked Chauncey as she put an empty plate in front of him.

"It was great. A lot of lives were changed," Chauncey replied.

"We have a men's retreat at my church," Tory offered.

"You should attend our retreats. They are off the chain. Is that what the kids say?" Chauncey looked around the table for confirmation.

"That's not what the kids say," Nicole replied as she took a seat.

"That sounds so powerful. A bunch of men getting together to worship God," Rachel mused.

Chauncey liked the soft tone of Rachel's voice. She sounded like a woman he could listen to for hours without getting bored. "It is definitely a powerful event, and as a deacon, you're pleased whenever lives are changed."

Nicole rolled her eyes at Chauncey, and Chauncey gave his baby sister a wink.

"That is awesome that you're a deacon. Wow." Rachel's eyes conveyed amazement.

"The food should be ready." Nicole got up and headed for the kitchen.

"I'll help." Rachel got up and followed Nicole into the kitchen.

Chauncey's eyes followed Rachel into the kitchen. Chauncey felt Tory's eyes follow him.

"Doesn't the Bible say that if you look at a woman lustfully, you've sinned?" Tory said.

"I haven't sinned. I've just admired God's greatest creation." Chauncey's eyes stayed fixed on the kitchen.

"You should write for Hallmark."

A few minutes later Nicole and Rachel emerged from the kitchen. Rachel carried a serving bowl filled with a chopped salad and a plate full of dinner rolls. Nicole followed behind Rachel with a steamy pot roast. Rachel sat the salad and rolls down next to an assortment of wines and wineglasses, then took her seat next to Chauncey.

"I hope you guys are hungry." Nicole sat the pot roast down in the middle of the table.

Chauncey leaned in to take a whiff of the roast. "Sis, I know you put your foot in this roast."

Tory reached across the table and grabbed a dinner roll and took a barbarian-like bite into the roll.

"Aren't you going to pray before you eat?" Chauncey asked Tory, who was fully engaged in consuming his dinner roll.

"I pray without ceasing." Tory put his roll on a napkin. "But I'll go ahead and lead us in prayer if it pleases you." Tory bowed his head like a knight. "God is great, and God is good."

Chauncey could not help but let out a chuckle at Tory's rudimentary prayer. He felt a sharp pain in his shin and knew that Nicole had just kicked him.

"Thank you for this food and amen," Tory said.

"Father, I just want to come to you and thank you for these blessings and gifts. I know that you are Jehovah-Jireh, our provider. Bless those who are less fortunate and those little kids in Africa that have no food, Lord," Chauncey said. "And those homeless kids by the Staples Center that have no shoes, Lord. And bless this food my sister, Nicole, prepared, and I pray that there's not too much salt and garlic to cause us to become ill." Chauncey felt another sharp kick to his shin and decided to conclude his prayer. "Amen."

Chauncey put a napkin over his shirt. "I'm sorry, Tory. I just wanted to make sure we had enough on the prayer for it to get through. I mean, if you don't have enough postage, your letter won't get to its destination."

"No problem," Tory said as he started to eat.

Chauncey watched Nicole feed Tory some of her food, which Chauncey could not understand, because everyone had the same thing on their plate. Maybe it was Nicole's way of showing affection, or maybe she had added something different to her food and she wanted Tory to try it.

In any case, Chauncey lost his appetite while he watched his sister act like a silly high school girl. He focused his attention on Rachel, who sat at the table with her head down. She ate her food like she did not want to be noticed or disturbed. She glanced up and greeted Chauncey's stare with a smile.

"You have amazing skin," Chauncey said.

"Thank you very much." Rachel launched into a detailed account of the oils and lotions she used.

"So what church do you go to?" Chauncey asked Rachel.

"I don't really go to church, but I do watch that guy who smiles a lot on TV. I like him!" Rachel replied.

"Oh, Lawd! Well, there's nothing like being in the presence of God. There's fullness of joy that you can't get from home," Chauncey said.

"But isn't God everywhere?" Rachel asked.

Tory nearly choked on his food at Rachel's valid point.

"So, Tory, I never got a chance to ask you what church you go to," Chauncey said with a smirk.

"I go to the same church as Nicole."

"Well, that's unfortunate," Chauncey replied.

"Chauncey." Nicole cut her eyes at Chauncey.

Tory frowned. "How's that? We study from the same Bible, and we believe that Jesus is our Lord and Savior."

"We all have our unique way of worshipping God," Nicole interjected.

"Yeah, but if it don't line up with the Word, then it ain't from God," Chauncey argued.

"Look, you can believe what you want to believe, and I'll believe what I believe," Tory responded.

"I believe in the Bible. I don't know what philosophy or doctrine you believe in, but it ain't the Word," Chauncey said.

"My mother always taught me that we're all looking at the same building, just from different angles," Rachel replied. "It's the same God, just different viewpoints."

"Your mom must love Chinese food, because that sounds like fortune-cookie wisdom to me," Chauncey said.

Chauncey was certain his comment would offend Rachel, but instead she burst out in laughter. Her laughter provided instant warmth to Chauncey. In spite of her beliefs, Chauncey attraction to Rachel was not severed.

Tory took Nicole's hand and kissed it. "You look real beautiful tonight, and dinner was excellent."

"Thanks, sweetie. Why don't you go into the living room and watch the game while I get dessert ready?"

"Sounds good." Tory gave Nicole another kiss on the hand.

It did not, however, sound good to Chauncey, who tasted the sourness of his meal in his throat.

"Chauncey!" Nicole slapped the table and gave Chauncey a head gesture in the direction of the kitchen.

"Excuse me," Chauncey said to Rachel, who gave him a smile before she went back to her meal.

He knew he'd struck a nerve with his sister. She wore aggravation on her face. Chauncey was reluctant, but he got up and followed his sister into the kitchen, where the sound of the football game coming from the living room would muffle their conversation.

"Do you ever wonder why you're single?" Nicole asked.

"You could've told me that you were trying to fix me up," Chauncey replied.

"I figured you needed help after the last date you told me about."

"Any kids?"

"No," Nicole said.

"Good credit score?" Chauncey asked, to which Nicole did a "so-so" hand gesture. "But she isn't saved." Chauncey looked back at Rachel, who had her head down again.

"Go slow. She's had a rough life, and she wants to believe in God, but it's hard for her. You could maybe get her to change her mind if you ease off the criticism."

Chauncey's head told him to stay far away from a nonbeliever. His heart did not want him to give up on Rachel so easily. "There's something about her that I can't deny."

"You never know what God may have in store for both of you."

"You may be right." Chauncey glanced back at Rachel.

"Now, why are you trying to ruin things between me and Tory?" Nicole shoved the dishes into the sink.

"You can't tell me he's what God has for you! The man don't even go to church."

"He's not perfect, but at least he's honest."

"There's some honest atheists that are going straight to hell."

Nicole grabbed the trash can from under the sink and took one of the plates she'd previously shoved into the sink. She slid the remaining food on the plate into the trash can before placing the plate back into the sink.

"If you would give people a chance, you'd be amazed at how wonderful and similar people are," Nicole said.

"I just don't think he's right for you. I think your clock is ticking and you're settling. I mean, I don't know how else to put it."

"You know what I think? I think you're jealous of me," Nicole said as she took a strawberry cheesecake out of the refrigerator.

"What do I have to be jealous of? You and nursery rhymes Tory?"

"You're jealous that I found somebody, and you're afraid that you're going to lose me, because I'm all that you have left."

"So long as I got King Jesus, I'm going to be okay. You want to wreck your life? Go ahead, but don't say that I didn't warn you."

Nicole made a choking gesture toward Chauncey and grunted. "God, you can be so stubborn at times. Wake up, Chauncey. Life moves on. I loved Henry, and I was with him to the end, but it's time to move on and for me to be happy. You can't smother me because you're afraid that you're going to lose me, like you lost Henry."

"You know what? You're really lost and confused, and you're not making any sense right now. I'm going to go," Chauncey said before he let out a grunt.

Chauncey stormed out of the kitchen. Rachel hopped up from the dining-room table and tried to cut him off at the pass. "Hey, listen, I was wondering if we could go out sometime."

Chauncey stopped dead in his tracks. "I would like that very much. How about you come with me to church on Sunday?"

"I was thinking more like a movie."

Chauncey did not like to go to the movies, but Rachel's appeal was too much for him to resist. "Sure!"

"Great! Let's go Saturday." Rachel went and grabbed her purse from her chair and came back with a cell phone in hand. "Give me your phone number."

Chauncey exchanged phone numbers with Rachel and wondered if he could resist her appeal. She had already got Chauncey to go on a date to the movies. He wondered what else Rachel could persuade him to do.

# Chapter Twenty-eight

## *Jamal*

*Two Months after the Retreat and Four Weeks until the Wedding . . .*

As if playing a game of who could be quiet the longest, Chantel and Jamal sat in silence. Chantel was not known for being short on words, at least not from Jamal's perspective, even she was speechless. But Jamal knew that Pastor Brown had plenty to say, and yet he sat in his office chair with his hand over his mouth and his index finger on his temple, reminiscent of Malcolm X. Pastor Brown's smile bordered on curiosity and condescension.

"So, Pastor, how was your weekend?" Jamal asked.

"It was fine, but we're not here for me. We're here for you and Chantel." Now Pastor Brown's smile moved into full-blown sardonic mode.

"What, Pastor?" Jamal shrugged his shoulders.

"I just find it amazing how comfortable we are when it comes to talking about sex and even having sex, until we get here." Pastor Brown pointed at his oak table. "And here is where we find a purpose for sex that supersedes animal cravings."

Jamal felt a lot more relaxed after Pastor Brown addressed the elephant in the room. He had simultaneously looked forward to and dreaded the session on sex. A discussion with his pastor and his fiancée about his desired marital sex life did not bring comfort to Jamal. He likened the experience to that of a teenage couple engaged in a discussion with their parents about their desires to havesex. At the same time, Jamal doubted that he and Chantel could have a successful marriage if their sex life left little to be desired. Therefore, he had looked forward to the opportunity to address their sexual expectations in terms of God.

"I'm not going to lie to you. I'm not comfortable talking about sex with you," Chantel said to Pastor Brown.

"Then don't look at me. Look at the Bible, because that is where my advice is coming from." Pastor Brown shrugged his shoulders.

"That's my whole problem, Pastor." Jamal started a balancing act with his hands. "Sex and the Bible don't seem to go together. I mean, the Bible talks about living holy, and at least for me, sex is freaky. I can't get in the mood for sex listening to Shirley Caesar."

That statement sparked a chuckle from Pastor Brown, and Chantel shook her head in presumed embarrassment.

"Seriously, though, I'm just trying to keep it one hundred with you, Pastor," Jamal continued. "What if I was into handcuffs and peanut butter? How would that be okay in the Bible?"

Chantel rolled both her head and her neck in shock. "I ain't no porn star. Let's get that straight. I'm not going to walk around in a French maid outfit or take pole-dancing classes."

"I can't think of one man who wouldn't want a woman that can be a lady in public and a freak in the bedroom," Jamal replied.

"That is very profound. Show me where that insight is located in the scriptures." Pastor Brown pointed to the open Bible on his desk.

"Yeah, Jamal. Show me where that is in the Bible," Chantel said as she picked up Pastor Brown's Bible and started to turn the pages.

"It's not in scripture, but there has to be a level of carnality in marriage. I mean, last time I checked, there's no sex in heaven. Am I right?" Jamal asked Pastor Brown.

"There is a level of carnality, but you have to decide whether or not you are going to have God at the center of your marriage or the world." Pastor Brown was silent for a minute. "I've seen a lot of marriages crumble because of selfishness and because the couples opened doors in their marriages that they couldn't close."

"That's what I'm wondering, Pastor, what's really off-limits. And can you be a married couple and still sin when it comes to sex?" Jamal thought he had asked Pastor Brown a tough question, but Pastor Brown seemed unfazed by it.

"Sex comes down to intimacy and, let's admit it, vulnerability. People who only see sex as passion and pleasure miss the intent."

Jamal hoped the way he contorted his face would convey his need for clarity from Pastor Brown.

"Let me ask you guys something. Would you have sex in a public place?" Pastor Brown asked.

Jamal and Chantel looked at each other and grumbled. Both of them had delved into exhibitionism on occasion.

"Wow. Okay, I'm just going to move on to my point." Pastor Brown sat up in his chair. "God's perfect will is for both husband and wife to desire only each other. Imagine if you made love to your spouse without thinking about an ex-boyfriend or ex-girlfriend or a porn star or Meagan Good. Imagine how much more closer you would draw toward God and each other if nothing stood in your way."

Pastor Brown paused for a moment, and Jamal allowed his statements to tumble around in his head. Jamal could tell that Pastor Brown's question had resonated with Chantel as well.

The pastor went on. "The point I'm trying to make is that ultimately it is up to you guys to determine the kind of sex life you will have, but if you open the door to the public and allow threesomes, adult movies, and everything else to become a necessity, then you'll find yourself in more trouble than you can handle."

"What about keeping the spice in the marriage?" Chantel asked.

"I say stick to the original recipe before someone steals your dish." Pastor Brown couldn't help but laugh. Chantel and Jamal joined in with a chuckle.

"Now that we got that settled, Chantel, how often do you plan to have sex with your husband in your marriage?" Pastor Brown asked.

"I don't know." Chantel shrugged her shoulders. "Three, maybe four times a week."

"A week!" Jamal said. "How about three or four times a day?"

"Oh, please." Chantel rolled her eyes.

"How often have you guys engaged in fornication in the time you have been together?" the pastor asked.

Chantel let out a deep sigh and put her head down as she began to rub her neck. Jamal started to twiddle his thumbs and let out a whistle.

"Come on now. If you want this thing to be right, you have to be open and honest," Pastor Brown urged.

"It's complicated," Chantel said.

"Love is never simple. People often see the complexities of love and marriage as a sign to abandon ship, when really they should be a sign that draws two people close together," Pastor Brown said.

"But you got to understand, Pastor, Chantel started off as my best friend's girlfriend, and then, after knowing each other for some time, we . . . we . . ." Jamal made a hand gesture in hopes that Pastor Brown would fill in the blank.

"Fornicated?" Pastor Brown said.

"Exactly!" Jamal snapped his fingers and pointed toward Pastor Brown. "And so much has happened as a result of that decision that I think it is hard for us to communicate and really forgive ourselves. I mean, my best friend would've never lost his cool that night, which led to him being killed, if it weren't for him finding out about me and Chantel having sex. And that weighs on me heavy, Pastor. I don't have a lot of regrets, but that's one that I do have."

Jamal put his head down because his mind had started to replay the night Clay died. "I wish he would've hit me instead of that guy. I would've taken that butt whupping. I owed him at least that for betraying him."

Chantel started to rub Jamal's back, and with her free hand, she wiped her eyes. Time healed all wounds, but in the few years that had passed since Clay's death, Jamal could not think about his fallen friend without an ache in his chest that snatched the wind out of him. The memory of Clay getting into a fight after Jamal confessed to having an affair with Chantel remained vivid. An altercation with a drunk knucklehead had led to Clay being murdered. Jamal had both mourned the loss of his best friend and harbored guilt about his death.

"Jamal, you can't carry that weight. You made your choice, and so did your friend. You're right. He could've taken it out on you instead of someone else, but you did not kill your friend," Pastor Brown said.

Jamal had heard that statement at least a hundred times, but it was hard for him to believe it was true. His actions had started a chain of events that led to the death of his best friend and and left a three-year-old-boy fatherless.

"What was it about her?" Pastor Brown leaned forward and pointed at Chantel.

Jamal leaned back in his chair and considered Pastor Brown's question. No one had ever asked that specific question. "I don't know. I mean, she was wifey material from the beginning, even in high school. I could tell that she was going to make some guy the happiest man on the planet. She's fine. She cooks, cleans, and is educated. My best friend was not treating her right. And you know the whole guys' code. I couldn't say anything to her, but I kept thinking that I should've been her man."

"What happened when you told your best friend?"

"He didn't take it too well. He got mad, got into a fight, and was later shot and killed. I was the last person that saw him alive. The coldest thing was that he died in a car with his best friend, who had just betrayed him."

A tear snuck out of Chantel's eye. It was still painful to recall the events that had led to Clay's downfall.

"You still have a lot of emotions there?" Pastor Brown handed Chantel a tissue from his tissue box on his desk.

"It's just that I feel like it's all my fault, and if I had just cut things off with Clay as soon as I started to get feelings for Jamal, things would've been different."

"So you don't regret your feelings for Jamal?" Pastor Brown asked.

Chantel used the tissue to keep back a stream of tears. "No. Even after all that has happened, I still love Jamal very much, and I don't want to be with anyone else."

"Where does your son, Jamir, fit in all of this?" Pastor Brown bounced his eyes from Chantel to Jamal as he waited for an answer.

"Jamir is my son. I would be lying if I told you that I don't sometimes wrestle with the fact that he's not my biological son, but I love him and I would do anything for him," Jamal revealed.

"Listen, nothing you do can change the past or undo what has already been done. You have to trust God and believe that He can restore all things."

Both Chantel and Jamal nodded in agreement. The tears receded and left red eyes in their wake. Jamal thought about the life that he wanted: a career, a wife, kids, a house and, above all, a great relationship with his Savior. These dreams at times appeared to be just within reach, and at other times they seemed more elusive than anything else.

"So what about now? Are you guys doing the right thing and waiting for marriage before you experience the fourth heaven?" Pastor Brown asked.

Jamal was usually reserved when it came to his sexual desires. He knew that if he was to open up about sex, then there would be a flood that he could not shut off.

"We were living together as you know, but I moved out right before the men's retreat," Jamal confessed.

Pastor Brown responded to Jamal's comment with a groan.

"Pastor, I know it was wrong, but it's difficult living in this economy. It's kind of cost-effective for two people who are going to get married to do what's economically feasible," Jamal explained.

"Once again I ask, who are you going to have at the center of your marriage? If you're going to serve God, then serve God. If you're going to go by the world and the economy, then there's no need for us to continue with these sessions."

Pastor Brown had given Jamal more than just food for thought. He had Jamal mull over the tough decisions he would have to make as the man of the house. Jamal did not want his stepson to think that he could play house without a spiritual commitment. Those thoughts stuck with Jamal after the session had concluded, and he broached them as he and Chantel walked back to the car.

"You're going to be the head of the household, so whatever you think is best, I will roll with it," Chantel said.

"What makes you say that?" Jamal opened the car door.

"I've had trust issues, but you've always been there and you've never given me a reason not to trust you." Chantel fanned her eyes.

"Chantel, I'm going to need you to trust God more. I'm human and I'm flawed, but God can give us a great marriage if we work at it."

"I agree," Chantel said as she got into the car.

Excitement and anxiety clashed within Jamal's psyche. Strong-willed Chantel would willingly give in and become submissive so that Jamal could be head of household. He felt anxiety because the success of the family now rested on his ability to heed God's directions. Jamal was not oblivious to the fact that this discussion continued all the way to their destination.

Jamal climbed in the car, and twenty minutes later they arrived at Clay's parents' house to find Clay's father, Gerald Atkins, standing outside the house with Jamir, who stood beside him with his Elmo backpack on. There was a clear contrast between Jamal's sun-kissed skin and Jamir's darker skin. Jamal's round cheekbones, which enhanced his smile, were quite different from Jamir's straight cheekbones.

To this day, Mr. Atkins had not taken the news well that his son was a victim of a foolish love triangle. He ushered Jamir along, and once Jamir reached Jamal's Honda, Mr. Atkins gave an about-face. He climbed up the short flight of steps that led from his walkway to his front porch and closed the front door behind him, giving every indication that he did not want to be bothered.

# Chapter Twenty-nine

### Chauncey

Since the dinner at Nicole's house, Chauncey and Rachel had not only talked over the phone, but had also chatted online on Facebook. Long phone conversations and online chats increased their anticipation of their first date.

"Two tickets for *Just Wright*," Chauncey said.

The young lady at the box office of the two-dollar movie theater handed him both his tickets and his change. Chauncey did not go to the movies often, because many of the movies that came out lacked substance and were vehicles for filth. Rachel had promised him that this movie was a quality black film and that he wouldn't have to worry about his salvation being in jeopardy. Chauncey trusted Rachel's judgment. There was something different about Rachel, and Chauncey couldn't figure out why he was drawn to her. It was more than the fact that Rachel was a natural beauty with skin as smooth and shiny as rich chocolate.

"You ready?" Chauncey asked.

"Ready." Rachel took Chauncey by the arm, and the whiff he got of her perfume sent a jolt of energy through his veins. "Ooh, popcorn! I got to have popcorn. It would be a sin not to have any popcorn."

Chauncey could not resist Rachel's childish joy as they strolled toward the concession stand, and he bought her a large popcorn and a Diet Coke. They made their way into a small theater, which was empty, and after securing their seats, Chauncey snatched a handful of popcorn and stuffed it in his mouth.

"Hey!" Rachel protested.

"Finder's fee," Chauncey said with a laugh.

"I used to love to go to the movies," Rachel said.

"I don't!" Chauncey had a sour look on his face.

"You don't go out much, do you? When was the last time you've been to the movies?"

"I saw the first *Matrix*," Chauncey replied

"Oh, that was my movie. When homegirl jumped and paused in the air? And Laurence Fishburne was a bad brother."

"Yeah, when that movie came out, that was the last time I went to the movies, because I knew that the Antichrist had arrived."

"Oh, I can't wait to hear this. Go ahead. Explain!" Rachel stuffed some popcorn in her mouth.

"You've got Neo pretending to be the Savior, rescuing people from slavery while doing kung fu."

"Did Jesus know kung fu?" Rachel asked.

"Of course He did. He's the Savior. He knows everything. He just didn't need to kick anybody in the face to prove it."

Rachel burst out into laughter and almost choked on her popcorn when she finished clearing her throat. She placed her hand on top of Chauncey's, and Chauncey felt the electricity flow from one hand to the other. Just then the previews started.

"You got to loosen up, Deacon. It's bad enough you're in a movie theater dressed like you're about to go to church."

Chauncey gave his beige suit with the orange collared shirt a once-over. He knew he was going to the movies, which was the reason why he didn't wear a tie. "Let me ask you something?"

"Shoot!" Rachel said in between bites of popcorn.

"Why don't you go to church?" Chauncey asked.

"It just seems like everybody is having a good time and is being entertained, and it feels like they already got their miracle. I never felt like God cared about me, which isn't hard, since I'm only one of six billion."

"But God does love you, and you're not insignificant."

"But sometimes I wake up and I feel so empty. I mean, I've had a lot of people who said they loved me, including God, and sometimes I feel like they've abandoned me."

"The devil is a liar! You're uniquely and wonderfully made. There are good people who would treat you with the respect you deserve."

"Yeah, but there's a shortage of good men available, and I figured my best chances were to meet a good churchgoing man."

Rachel's worldly mind-set baffled Chauncey. He gained a new level of understanding about the infamous proverb that urged him not to lean on his own understandings.

"Do you believe in God?" Chauncey asked.

"I do. I just don't think He's as picky as everyone makes Him out to be." Rachel stuffed more popcorn in her mouth.

"There's is only one God, and He's a jealous God."

"That's your interpretation. I went to a church where every week they made people go down to the altar and confess their sins. Everything you wore was a sin, and I got filled up with a lot of bad doctrine, to the point where I just stopped going. I figured if I was going to go to hell, I might as well have a little fun."

"There's nothing in hell you want," Chauncey said.

"Look, I've had a lot of disappointments in my life, and I don't believe a loving God would allow so much suffering."

Chauncey saw a beautiful young woman in front of him who was sweet and caring, but the trials of life had hardened her heart. While normally such statements as Rachel's would launch Chauncey into full evangelistic mode, he couldn't muster up the gumption to try and get Rachel saved.

"God loves you, Rachel, and I know that He desires for you to have a relationship with Him."

"You are really sweet, Chauncey. I'm glad that I'm here with you." Rachel nudged Chauncey with her elbow.

"So am I," Chauncey said, and to his surprise, that was not a lie. He did enjoy being in the presence of Rachel.

They sat in the movie theater, and despite Chauncey's initial resistance, he actually enjoyed the movie. He loosened up and realized that some movies were pretty good and entertaining, but Rachel's point of view on God was still disturbing.

# Chapter Thirty

## *Jamal*

Chantel laid the plates on top of the dining room table at a frantic pace. "God, we still got the lasagna in the oven, and I still have to get dressed."

"Don't worry. We still have time," Jamal said.

"That's easy for you to say. You men have it easy. It only takes you a minute to get ready." Chantel started to rub her head, searching her mind for anything that she might have forgotten to do. "This dinner thing was a bad idea."

"We're about to get married in a few short months. It's important for us to hang out with other married couples."

"Then why is Chauncey coming over?"

"Aren't you curious to see what Chauncey's girlfriend looks like?" Chantel shrugged her shoulders, and Jamal walked over and took the silverware that was in her hands. "Go ahead and get ready. I got this." It was a simple gesture that went a long way. Jamal had learned that the key to a woman's heart dwelled in being able to do the simple things that made her world easier.

"Thank you." Chantel wrapped her arms around Jamal and gave him a kiss. She made her way to the bedroom as Jamal continued to place silverware on the table.

A half an hour later, Quincy and Karen were the first to arrive. The women congregated in the kitchen, while Quincy and Jamal sat in front of the TV, watching the movie *Juice* on BET.

"Have you seen Chauncey's girl?" Quincy asked.

"Now, that's what I'm interested in seeing. Who can stand to date him? I love him, but your boy can be a bit much."

"You need to let go of what happened at the men's retreat," Quincy said. "You know how Chauncey is. He can be a little judgmental at times, but his heart is in the right place."

"I'm trying to, but what I don't need is any more judgment. I did the right thing. I moved out, and I'm trying to work things out with Chantel before the wedding."

Quincy nodded his understanding.

The doorbell rang, and Jamal knew that it was the moment of truth. Jamal and Quincy got up and made their way to the door. When they opened the door, they saw Chauncey with a Kool-Aid smile on his face and a woman of the same height next to him. The woman had a heart-shaped face and beautiful hazel eyes. Jamal was a little taken aback because he did not expect her to be so pretty, being she was interested in plain old Chauncey.

"You're too cute to be with an L-seven like this one," Quincy said and pointed at Chauncey.

"Brother Page, stop being a fool and move out of the way," Chauncey said, shaking his head.

Quincy moved out of the way and extended his hand like an usher. "All right, now, Deacon. I'll be darn."

Quincy and Jamal exchanged surprised looks before they chuckled to themselves.

\*\*\*

After dinner, the couples decided to play a game. What started out as a friendly game that would provide light exercise turned into an all-out war.

"Start it over," Quincy said, out of breath.

"Come on, Q. That was the tiebreaker," Jamal said, also out of breath.

"Baby, just let it go," Karen said while sitting on the couch next to Chantel. Both women had sweat on their face, and they clung to their bottles of water.

"Naw, naw, naw. The Page family does not lose. Now, start it over one more time."

"Brother Page, maybe we should do something that is more wholesome," Chauncey suggested. He and Rachel were the only ones that were not out of breath and sweating.

"Quiet. This doesn't concern you. Now, let's go. Bring it!" Quincy insisted.

Karen and Chantel got up and took their positions next to the men in their lives. Jamal handed everyone a Nintendo Wii remote and cued up the Michael Jackson game. All of a sudden the two couples were engaged in an intense battle over the song "Thriller."

Jamal tried to nail every move from the famous song with a perfect score, and he knew that he and Chantel were in sequence, which was how their marriage should unfold.

"Lord, have mercy," Chauncey said as he looked on.

# Chapter Thirty-one

## *Chauncey*

After the dinner, Rachel was quiet all the way home. Chauncey tried to figure out what he could have done wrong to offend Rachel, but he drew a blank. He pulled up to Rachel's home and turned off the car. He noticed that Rachel sat there as if she was unaware of the fact that they were parked outside of her home.

"Let me ask you something. What was the purpose of dinner tonight?" Rachel asked.

"I just wanted you to meet my friends."

"For what? I'm not saved, so in a minute you will probably dump me."

"I didn't say anything about dumping you." Chauncey was somewhat excited that Rachel was really concerned about the fate of their relationship.

"So you're willing to keep dating me even if I don't get saved?" Rachel rolled her neck.

"No. Don't get me wrong. I want you to get saved, but that was not the point of the evening."

"What was the point? Why can't we just be how we are? Having me meet your friends was not fair." Rachel leaned her head against the window in frustration.

"You didn't have a great time?" Chauncey asked.

"I had a great time. I really like your friends, and I want to spend more time with them. But if I'm not saved, then what's the point?"

"There is a point. I think we have something special, and I don't want it to end," Chauncey replied.

Rachel's eyes grew large, as if she had just won the lottery. "You don't even know me. We've dated only for a few weeks."

"That's why it's so frustrating. It's that I don't really know you, but I know that I would trade in everything but my salvation for you, a woman who makes me feel like you do inside."

"I wish I could believe blindly like you. But I can't. I have seen too much and have had a lot of bad stuff happen to me. There's a lot about me that you don't know about. You live in your little bubble at church, and you're closed off to a real world, where little girls get beaten and molested."

The way Rachel said that last statement, Chauncey did not have to guess who that little girl was. Chauncey searched for words that could convey empathy. "You can't go through life, Rachel, thinking that you're not worthy of being in love. I don't pity you. I pity your soul, because you have experienced so much pain and have not allowed God to heal you."

"It's a lot easier to deal with life when you feel numb in the heart. I'm sorry, but I don't need your charity and I don't need your pity. All I need is to get out of this car."

"Rachel . . ."

Rachel waved him off as she got out of the car.

Rachel was done talking, but Chauncey was not. He got out of the car and stood on the driver's side. "You're a hypocrite."

Rachel stopped and turned around, as if Chauncey had just called her out of her name. "Excuse me? What are you talking about?"

Chauncey wasn't sure what he was talking about. He had just wanted to stop Rachel in her tracks, and he'd succeeded.

"I said you're a hypocrite." Chauncey closed the door and walked to the front of the car.

"You got your nerves!" Rachel said.

"You want to talk about how you can't find a good man, and here I stand. Now, because I have a set of principles of what I expect from a woman, you want to criticize me? You're a hypocrite!"

"How can I ever measure up to the mighty Deacon Chauncey McClendon?" Rachel asked.

Chauncey could not explain what came over him. It was the way that Rachel's lips moved to form her words. Chauncey took a leap of faith and kissed Rachel. Chauncey imploded with desire, and Rachel did not pull back. She pulled Chauncey closer, and then he felt her replace her lips with her finger. He opened his eyes to see tears in Rachel's eyes. She removed her finger from his lips, turned, and walked away.

"Rachel." Chauncey couldn't muster up enough strength to say her name louder.

Chauncey did not know what had just transpired, but he knew that he needed to repent.

# Chapter Thirty-two

## *Titus*

Beethoven's "Ode to Joy" came from the satellite stereo and blended with the sound of the Range Rover's air-conditioning. Carlos was a valuable employee not only for his ability to navigate around Southern California, which allowed Titus to sit back and work on his sermons. Titus also valued Carlos's ability to put up with classical music, soft jazz, and occasional gospel music. Titus loved gospel music, but he found it hard to concentrate on his messages when music with lyrics was playing. Classical and jazz spoke without words, and Titus's mind was able to focus.

"Is it too cold in here, Pastor?" Carlos made eye contact with Titus through the rearview mirror.

"I'm good, Doc. Thank you," Titus said as he worked on his sermon notes on his iPad.

"We're here, Pastor," Carlos said as the truck came to a complete stop in the driveway.

Silver Brook Senior Community had the decor that one would expect of a luxury senior community. Its postmodern design, along with its pools, state-of-the-art fitness center, and community room, put most senior homes to shame. People paid at least thirty-five hundred a month so that their loved one could have both comfort and companionship.

"Thanks, Doc. Pull around the side. I shouldn't be long," Titus said as he grabbed the flower vase of Casa Blancas and exited the car.

"Will do, Pastor," Carlos said as the passenger door closed.

Titus walked through the double doors and rested the flowers on the reception desk as he signed in.

"How are you today, Pastor?" Tiffany, the afternoon receptionist, asked.

"I'm fine, Tiffany, and yourself?"

"I'm fine. Thank you for asking. She is in her room."

Titus gave Tiffany a wink, and she in return gave Titus a smile that brightened her mocha complexion. Titus grabbed the flowers and made a beeline through the community room, filled with elderly men and women engaged in an assortment of activities, from board games to reading to playing the grand piano. As Titus walked, he whistled "Ode to Joy," which was stuck in his head. Titus exited the community room and made his way down a long corridor of rooms until he arrived at 119. The door was always unlocked, but Titus knocked, anyway, as he opened the door.

"Hello, beautiful." Titus entered the room. He saw the forty-two-inch flat-screen TV on, but from his angle he could not see if anyone was on the couch.

"Come in, son," Victoria, Titus's mother, said.

Titus passed the kitchen counter, which blocked his view of his mother. He stopped near the TV to observe his mother, who sat on the couch with her legs crossed, as if she had been expecting him.

"What are you watching?" Titus asked as he looked back.

"Oprah's *Behind the Scenes*," Victoria said as she muted the TV.

"Here you go, Mom." Titus handed her the vase filled with Casa Blancas.

"Oh, you didn't have to do that. You gave me Casa Blancas for my birthday." Victoria took the vase and sat it right in front of her.

"Do I need a reason? The Casa Blanca is a rare, beautiful flower, just like a woman I know," Titus said as he reached into his pocket and removed a rectangular card in an envelope. "Here you go, Mom. Buy yourself something nice."

"Honey, I don't even go anywhere," Victoria replied.

"I know you have excursions. That's what I pay for." Titus had a seat on the couch next to his mother.

"I don't really go. I'm not that much into going out."

Titus wished that excuse would suffice, that it would explain his mother's absence on his wedding day. Titus considered himself a strong man, but he was not made of solid oak. The fact that his mother was not there during one of the most important moments of his life caused Titus to ache inside. God had waited until Titus was in his mid-forties to bring him Grace. God had waited for Titus to be ready to throw off the stigma of the past and embrace love. No matter how much Titus tried to rationalize his mother's actions, the word *why*, followed by a huge question, would come up.

"You want some coffee?" Victoria asked as she stood up.

"Sure. Let me help you with that." Titus stood up to give his mother a hand.

"Oh no, you make yours too sweet. I'll go into a diabetic coma." Victoria walked into the kitchen, and Titus walked over to the counter and rested his forearms on it.

"I saw Dad," Titus said.

Victoria stopped dead in her tracks. "Really? Where?"

"He showed up at the men's retreat to apologize."

For a moment, Victoria acted like she hadn't heard anything. She just continued to put fresh coffee in the dispenser of the coffeemaker Titus had bought her last Christmas. "I guess he decided to come back out here and take the senior pastor position."

When his father left, Titus knew about his whereabouts only through word of mouth, one of the disadvantages of being born in the precomputer age. "I thought I would never see him again."

"Son, your father is a pathological liar. If you haven't figured that out yet, then I don't know what to tell you."

The years had not reduced the disdain that Titus's mother had for his father. Titus still felt love for his father, no matter how much he tried to suppress his feelings.

"Did he ask about me?" Victoria asked.

Titus could only shake his head. His mother acted like she didn't care, but the truth was, it hurt her that Lemont did not ask about her.

"I think he knows not to come within fifty feet of me," Victoria continued.

"Do you forgive him?" Titus asked.

"How's Grace?" Victoria tried to change the subject.

"Do you really want to talk about Grace?" Titus asked.

Victoria stopped midway through taking the coffee cups off the counter. "Why would you say that?"

"Because we're not talking about Grace."

"Well, I don't want to talk about your father, okay!" Victoria brought her fists down on the counter like a hammer.

"Mom, since I told you that I met someone, you have met Grace only once, and you haven't inquired about her, other than asking how she is. Grace is my wife, not some stranger."

"You're still mad about the wedding. I told you that I wasn't feeling well, and I'm sorry that I couldn't make it." Victoria slammed the cups down on the counter.

"Mom, I know you. We took care of each other when Dad left. I know you didn't want me to become a preacher, but I did, and I can't understand why you're not happy for me."

Victoria did not respond immediately. She just poured black coffee into the two cups and went into the refrigerator to grab cream and sugar.

"It's hard for me to be happy for you when I can see down the road." Victoria returned to the counter and began to mix cream and sugar into the coffees. "Your father and I were together for less than four months when we got married. He was the talk of the town, like you, only you've gone a lot farther than any other Dawkins male. I can imagine that Grace feels like how I felt, the envy of all women." Victoria handed Titus his coffee.

"Thank you," Titus said as he sat the coffee on the counter to cool. "Grace has been getting the cold shoulder from the sistas. I've lost some members as a result of my marriage."

Victoria was quiet, as if a thief had stolen her tongue. She pointed at Titus in an accusatory manner. Finally, she said, "I hear Lemont in that. I hear him. Lord Jesus, please protect my son."

"I'm nothing like my father. The devil is a liar," Titus replied.

"Yeah, and you're lying to yourself if you think you're not. Don't be foolish and think you're above the same failings as your father and the other men in this family. You have to confront it and pray that God will drive it out of you."

A chill swept over Titus. His mother was not the reserved, graceful woman he had always known. She had turned into a profit of doom, and Titus wondered if he was doomed.

"I took one look at Grace, and I saw the woman I used to be. I used to be hopeful, happy, and loving. Your father and that church bled all of that out of me, and now I'm all alone," Victoria said, her voice cracking.

"You're never alone. You have God, and you have me."

"I have God, and I have you when your schedule is open. In the end I fear that when God calls me home, you'll be somewhere halfway across the world, preaching. Let me tell you this. If you don't put your wife first, ahead of that church, then you're no better than your father!"

Victoria's words made a home in Titus's psyche. The outward displays of disrespect toward Grace from the women of the church were unacceptable. Mysterious phone calls throughout the night were all a sign that Titus needed to regain control of the situation. Titus knew exactly where to go.


The sanctuary of Greater Anointing was empty with the exception of a few dozen women who filled out the first few rows. Titus sat beside Grace as they faced the small group of women.

The reason for the gathering was simple. The event was supposed to be a girl talk hosted by First Lady Grace, and the attendance reflected just how much the women of the congregation wanted to spend quality time with Grace. To everyone's surprise, Titus was present, and he knew that some of the first lady's biggest detractors would be present as well. This event would give them something to talk about.

"I feel like this was long overdue," Grace said before she cleared her throat. "I wanted to talk with you ladies and get a chance to be real and talk about how you feel and how we can make Greater Anointing a much more inviting place."

"I've always felt like Greater Anointing was a very inviting place," Tamika said.

Grace begged to differ. "Well, I have to be honest. I didn't get that kind of feeling."

"That's because . . . You know what? Let me be quiet." Tamika put her hands over her mouth.

"It's okay, sister. Say what's on your mind, because I'm going to do the same," Grace said.

"We are a church family, and you know that with a family you can say what's on your mind," Titus said as he took Grace by the hand.

"I'm just saying, this is our pastor and I love him like a father, and all of a sudden you came out of nowhere and up and married him," Tamika said to a chorus of head nods in agreement.

There was no turning back. Tamika had laid her cards on the table, and it looked as if everyone else held similar cards. Grace had to walk a fine line between delicate and firm.

"So you feel like I took your pastor away from you?" Grace asked.

Tamika shook her head. "Not like that. I'm just saying that we always felt like if Pastor was going to get married, it would be to one of the women from Greater Anointing. And when he married you, someone from another church, it was like saying that we weren't good enough."

"Of course you're good enough, and finding my husband at a men's retreat was the last thing on my mind. But I was open to what God had for me and not to what I wanted for myself. You have to do the same. God has an awesome man for you, and he'll be a better man for you than my husband could ever be, because he will be the one chosen especially for you," Grace replied.

Tamika wiped both the tears and the bitterness from her eyes. Titus didn't want to hurt anyone, and it pained him that some women felt inadequate because he didn't marry them.

"I just have a problem with not being able to have access to my pastor like I used to," Sister Pam said.

"Well, last I checked, Pastor still has office hours and that has not changed," Grace said.

"I know, but sometimes, in the middle of the night, I been going through it and I need to call—"

"Oh, Jesus!" Grace said, and some of the women chuckled.

"Sister Pam, you're one of my most faithful members, and I appreciate that, but that doesn't mean that you have round-the-clock access to me. I need time for myself and time to spend with my wife," Titus said.

"I just wish you would preach more, because some of these other ministers you got up here, uh-uh." Paula contorted her face, as if she had just eaten something sour.

"Every minister I bring up here has been handpicked by God, and He's a better judge of character than I am. There's a Word that could minister to you in every sermon, but you have to stop looking at the messenger and start listening to the message. God forbid I might make a colossal mistake and fall flat on my face. What are you going to do then? If you have a healthy belief system, then you'll probably pray for me and pick me up. If you don't have a healthy belief system, then you're going to move on to the next hot new pastor, who seems to walk on water but is really human." Titus paused to take a sip of cold water, allowing it to run down his dry throat.

He went on. "And another thing. This is my wife, and she's not going anywhere. Regardless of how you feel about my marriage, I expect all of you to give the first lady the respect she deserves. That means not walking past her on Sunday mornings after service without speaking. That means speaking to her and being respectful, because she has been respectful to all of you."

To Titus's surprise, he received an "amen" from the women. He was impressed by the way Grace handled herself. For the rest of the event she took questions and answered them with ease. She was not rattled by the criticism she drew from some of the members. Titus believed that his wife realized that the criticism was based on an assumption. It was not steeped in fact. Did this event mean the end of the conflict between Grace and some of the women in the church? Probably not, but the two sides had made a lot of headway. Titus was grateful to God that his house was no longer divided.

# Chapter Thirty-three

## Chauncey

Chauncey thought only of Rachel. At a moment that he had worked extremely hard for, Chauncey had found something that superseded the minister's exam: Rachel. The exam was a test of his knowledge of the scriptures, and Chauncey knew the Bible backward and forward, but he couldn't get his thoughts to stray away from Rachel. He wanted to call her, but he felt that after twenty voice mail messages, one more would earn him a restraining order.

Chauncey saw Rachel as neither a distraction nor a hindrance. She was who she was, a woman that had rocked Chauncey and his belief system to the core. It was not fair that Chauncey had met a woman who personified everything that he wanted in a wife and yet she did not want to speak to him. Was it really his destiny to remain single? Chauncey had never questioned God or his will, but he prayed that it was not God's will for him to walk alone for the rest of this life. Chauncey was ready to take a leap of faith, and he was willing to take a leap with Rachel. He just needed her to realize that only God could heal her wounds.

"Twenty minutes," Minister Angela said as she fulfilled her official capacity as the exam proctor.

Chauncey snapped out of his Rachel fixation long enough to look down at his exam and realize that he still had fifteen questions left. That would not have been a problem for Chauncey, except he could not focus, and this exam did not seem that important now that he had received an invitation to the ministers' class.

Chauncey tried to focus on his next question, which was for him to name the twelve tribes of Israel. Chauncey was halfway down the list when his phone started to vibrate. He tried to pretend that it was not his phone that was vibrating, but his tight-fitting gray slacks gave him away as Minister Angela peeked through her glasses at him. The phone stopped vibrating for a moment and then started again. Chauncey was embarrassed, but he figure that whoever was trying to get ahold of him was not about to stop calling.

"Hello?" He answered the phone in a whisper as he exited the exam room.

"Hi. Chauncey? This is Tanya. I'm Rachel's cousin, and I got your number from her phone," a woman said in a frantic tone.

"What's wrong?"

"Rachel was in a real bad car accident, and she was rushed to St. Joseph's Hospital and . . ."

Chauncey heard the words *Rachel, car accident,* and *St. Joseph's Hospital,* but the rest of the conversation got muffled. "I'm on my way."

Chauncey ended the call and rushed back into the exam room and gathered his coat. He would die if for the second time he was not there when someone needed him.

"Brother McClendon, where are you going?" Minister Angela asked.

"I've got to go."

"But you can't leave in the middle of the exam."

"Lord, forgive me, but I don't care."

Chauncey shot out of the church and hopped in his Cadillac. He prayed that he would not get pulled over for going seventy miles per hour in a sixty-five-mile-per-hour zone. During the drive, Chauncey prayed several other prayers, both out loud and to himself. He did not want to lose Rachel. She was so precious that one of his prayers was that God would allow him to suffer hardship in her stead.

Chauncey arrived at the hospital and made his way to the emergency room. He was familiar with the hospital because it was the same hospital that his brother, Henry, had died in. Chauncey kept a quick pace up the walkway and made his way through the double doors. He scanned the lobby, looking for anyone who could point him in the right direction. He made his way to the front desk, where the receptionist was doing data entry into the computer.

"I'm looking for a girl named Rachel!" Chauncey said.

"Chauncey!" a woman called, and when Chauncey turned around, he assumed that the woman was Tanya, Rachel's cousin, by her voice.

Chauncey made a beeline toward her, but then a man who was a giant stood up and stepped in front of her.

"Is this the guy who's responsible?" the man asked and started to make his way toward Chauncey.

The man was dressed in a mechanic's suit. The grease on his hands was not what made Chauncey nervous. It was the fact that his hands were balled up, as if the man had the intention to strike. Chauncey could not explain from where the urge arose within him, but he felt his fists ball up and had a desire to go to war.

The man drew closer, and all of a sudden Chauncey turned into the Terminator and infrared circles fired off in his mind and he saw a clear target. When the guy got within striking distance, Chauncey remembered what Will had shown him a while back. Chauncey cocked his hand back and let it fly. His fist landed on the guy's nose, and both of them hollered in pain. The guy grabbed his nose and held it, and Chauncey felt a sharp pain in his hand.

"Oh my God!" Chauncey said.

"Hey, man, what is wrong with you?" the guy asked.

"I thought you were going to attack me," Chauncey replied.

"No, I was going to give you a hug. Rachel thinks very highly of you. I don't know why now. What's wrong with you?" the man said, his hands still covering his nose.

"I'm so sorry. I am so sorry."

"I didn't know my cousin was dating a thug!" Tanya said when she reached them.

"I'm not a thug. I'm a deacon," Chauncey insisted.

"What kind of a church you go to?" Tanya and the guy said in unison.

Chauncey thought about lying and making up some church to avoid bringing shame to the house of Greater Anointing.

"I'm going to press charges on you," the guy said.

"Oh, Lord Jesus. No, Jesus," Chauncey said at the thought that he could be going to jail.

"Oh, Clyde, you watch boxing. Protect yourself at all times," Tanya said.

"Is there a problem?" the security guard asked. He'd abandoned his post outside the ICU.

"No, sir. Everything is fine," Tanya said before she gave the guy, Clyde, a pop on the head.

The security guard went back to his post outside the ICU.

"What happened?" Chauncey asked after the security guard left.

"She was really upset about the argument you two had last night, and I just think she wasn't paying attention while going to work today. She slid into the back of a car. The car was badly damaged," Tanya said.

"Why would she do that?" Chauncey asked.

"For a deacon you're not very perceptive, are you?" Clyde said.

"You're all she talks about. She talks about how smart you are, how funny, how spiritual, and how handsome you are. I mean, she really cares about you." Tanya looked Chauncey up and down.

That marked the first time Chauncey had ever heard a woman speak so highly of him. He regretted the argument that he and Rachel had had, and prayed that he would have a chance to make things right with her.

A nurse approached them, and she made eye contact with Tanya.

"Is she okay?" Tanya asked the nurse.

"She's stable. We're letting her get some rest and periodically checking in on her to make sure she is okay."

"Can I see her?" Chauncey asked.

"In a little while. Right now she's resting," the nurse said.

Chauncey took a seat in the waiting room and started to pray. *Lord, I pray right now for your mercy and your strength. Please allow Rachel to have a full recovery. And when she comes out, let her know that it is because of You and You alone that she made it through.*

Chauncey continued to pray for what must've been hours, because when he looked up, the day had retired and the night was in full bloom. Clyde, Tanya's husband, was watching sports highlights on the TV in the waiting room. Tanya sat there half asleep. Chauncey headed to the nurses' station.

"Is there any news?"

The nurse checked on her computer. "She has been moved to the fourth floor, to room four-twelve. You can go see her now," the nurse said.

"Okay. Thank you," Chauncey told the nurse before returning to the waiting room and sharing the news with Tanya and Clyde.

"Chauncey, why don't you go ahead and see her first? I'm sure she would like that," Tanya said before she yawned.

No man on earth could convince Chauncey that God did not answer prayer. Without hesitation he made his way to the elevator and headed to the fourth floor. When Chauncey arrived on the fourth floor, he searched for room 412. His heart rate increased when he saw the room. He wondered if Rachel would be awake or asleep.

Chauncey walked into the hospital room, and as he expected, Rachel was asleep. He took a seat next to her bed, and his heart started to ache at the sight of the woman that he was drawn to with IVs in her arm and connected to a machine. Chauncey was moved to pray again, but this time he touched her warm hand and knew that God would bring her out of this valley. He prayed until he saw Rachel's eyes open.

"I knew you would come," Rachel said with tears in her eyes.

"Of course. I'm not going to leave your side."

"But what about the ministers' class?"

"I've found something more important."

"But all you ever wanted to be was a minister. That's all you've talked about," Rachel said.

"I just wanted to feel important. I thought being a minister would make me important, but I didn't real-ize that I was something special this whole time. I allowed selfishness and ambition to cause a strain in my relationship with my family. But there is nothing more important than being here with you." Rachel could not hold back the tears, and Chauncey comforted her with a kiss on the forehead. "I love you!"

"I love you too, Chauncey, and I want to be with you. I prayed to God to give me another chance with you, and He has answered my prayer of finding love."

Chauncey was overwhelmed to hear Rachel say that she loved him. He knew that he was not an easy person to love, so for Rachel to love him willingly was amazing.

"I'm sorry about the other night. I've got a tendency to be a little high and mighty," Chauncey said.

"I know, but I love you, anyway," Rachel said as she winced from trying to sit up. Chauncey helped her adjust her position. "I want to come to church with you when I get out."

Chauncey leaned in and put his forehead gently against Rachel's and prayed with her. Chauncey was ready to take a leap of faith, and Rachel seemed to be ready to take that leap with him.

# Chapter Thirty-four

## *Quincy*

The retreat revealed a lot of lingering issues that Quincy thought a year of refocusing and renewed passions had resolved. He now accepted the fact that he had set his standards too high for Sasha. She was a bright girl, but everyone was capable of folly, and everyone needed a chance to better themselves. Sasha had decided not to return to school until after she had the baby. For Quincy, it was another twist of the knife, but a wise decision. College was a stressful environment, and being pregnant with a full load of courses was too much. Quincy planned to take Sasha back to school to clean out her apartment.

The weekend revealed to Quincy that Dwight was scared, but he was not a malicious person who never intended to have a serious relationship with his daughter. They both had acted stupidly and irresponsibly, but when it came to the child that they had conceived, they could not afford to be irresponsible. The stakes were too high.

Quincy could not say that he was ready to embrace the next chapter in his life, being a grandparent. He felt he had too much swagger to be a grandpappy. Of course, Quincy envisioned that twenty years down the road, he would still have more swag than the average man.

Given Quincy's inner turmoil, he had wanted to ditch the original plan of going to Palm Springs and instead pilot a G-V jet and go to Vegas. Jamal had given Quincy the honor of planning his bachelor party, or at least Quincy had given Jamal the honor of accepting his request to plan the bachelor party. In the end Quincy decided that Palm Springs was a great place to hold the event.

Recent revelations had made Quincy feel anything but festive. It was hard to have a different frame of mind when the body still served as a reminder of the pleasures it had once endured. Quincy lived between extremes. It was an innate personality trait of his to see things as either black or white, no in between. But the journey from the wrong way of living and thinking to the right way of living had left him in a dangerous middle ground that could go either way. Quincy found solace within the confines of his office.

Karen did her usual knock on the door and entered without waiting for Quincy to say "Come in."

"Baby, I don't know about you going out with the guys. I know it is the guys, but I' m worried about you," she said.

"Who knows? Maybe I might meet Sasha's baby daddy out there. You know, instead of worrying about me, maybe you should be more concerned with your daughter, who left this house, as well as her standards, behind."

"Don't get defensive."

"What do you expect? The women in this house do whatever they want, and they have the audacity to come at me sideways for wanting to have a little relief."

"You've come too far to mess up now."

"Don't preach to me. You have my heart, but you have no idea what my soul has been through and how tired I am of trying to walk right despite getting kneed in the gut."

Karen embraced Quincy. Her embrace was warm and genuine, and Quincy could not reject his wife.

"This isn't easy for me or for Sasha. She knows what she's done, but we have to be there for her. I just don't want to lose you in the process."

"You won't. I just want to go out with my guys and have fun."

"Promise me that you won't drink." Karen pointed her finger like a concerned parent.

"Promise!"

"Oh my God!" Sasha yelled from downstairs.

Paternal instinct kicked in, and Quincy shot down the steps and felt Karen hot on his heels. The image downstairs started off blurred, but as Quincy got closer, he clearly saw Sasha, and there was Dwight on one knee with an embarrassingly small ring in his hands.

"Oh my . . . " Karen said from behind Quincy.

"God!" Quincy added.

Quincy watched as Sasha's emotions attacked her nervous system and she cried to the point where she started to shake. A closer examination brought Quincy to the realization that Sasha's tears were not of joy.

"I love you, baby, and I want to be a good man and a good father. I want to spoil you and my baby," Dwight said.

Quincy applauded Dwight for his resolution to be a better man. He still wished he had never met Dwight, but Quincy was starting to like him.

"I'm sorry." Sasha bolted upstairs and slammed her bedroom door.

"I'll go talk to her." Karen did a light jog up the stairs.

Quincy was left with a shocked Dwight, who was still on one knee with the ring. He couldn't wrap his head around what had just happened.

"Well, you might as well get off that knee and come into the living," Quincy said with his hands in his pockets as he walked into the living room.

Quincy entered his living room and plopped down on his couch. Dwight had a seat next to him. The Thursday night football game was already in progress, and the Steelers were dominating, as usual.

"That's not the response I expected," Dwight said, finally finding his voice.

"Rarely is anything in life what we expect," Dwight said.

"Quincy," Karen shouted from the staircase.

"I'll be back. Sit tight, okay?" Quincy asked, and Dwight nodded.

Quincy got up and walked out of his living room and up the stairs to Karen, who almost seemed upset at him. "What is it?"

Karen did a hand gesture to silence Quincy. "Just go inside." Karen pointed at Sasha's room.

Quincy entered Sasha's room, and Sasha was still in tears. Despite his brilliant analytical mind, Quincy did not know why Sasha was crying.

"Baby girl, what's wrong?" Quincy asked.

"I really messed up," Sasha said between sobs.

Quincy wanted to congratulate his daughter on having a firm grasp on the obvious. He should've rejoiced in Sasha's revelation, but something told him that she was not done with her confessions.

"You don't want to marry Dwight?" Quincy asked.

"No, I do, but I just can't lie to him anymore." Sasha buried her face in her hands.

Quincy did not like where this conversation was headed, and a coldness swept through his body.

"When I first came back to school, Dwight and I were having a lot of problems, and I got the suspicion that since I had gone home for the summer, maybe he had found someone else. So one night, after a bad argument, I went out with my friends and met a guy." Sasha sobbed even more.

Quincy started to lose his sense of balance.

"Dad, we didn't use protection," Sasha bellowed.

A sudden burst of rage came over Quincy, and he kept the desire to haul off and slap Sasha at bay with a small amount of self-control. This could not be his daughter, to whom he had given every advantage in life. He now knew that there was a possibility that Dwight was not the father.

"Have you lost your mind?" Quincy asked.

Sasha responded with more sobs. "Mom, can you tell Dwight that I'm not feeling well and I'll call him later?"

Karen, who had quietly entered the room, went to speak, and Quincy put up his hand to silence her. "No. You're an adult, and we raised you to take responsibility for your actions and own up to your mistakes. Now, you go down there and you tell that boy the truth."

"Dad." Sasha could barely get the word out.

Quincy put his hand up to stop her and pointed to the door. He closed his eyes, because at that moment he could not stand the sight of his own daughter. When Quincy opened his eyes, Sasha was no longer in the room. Karen remained, equally bewildered.

"What is going on?" Quincy asked.

"Be cool, Quincy," Karen replied.

"I've been *too* cool. That's the problem. Our daughter done went off to college and became a liar and a wh—" Quincy bit his tongue.

A door downstairs slammed, which was not a shock to Quincy. He walked out of the room and made his way to the top of the staircase. He looked down and saw Sasha at the bottom of the stairs. Sasha was still crying, but for another reason. She had lost a guy who was on the verge of transformation.

# Chapter Thirty-five

## *Will*

*Two Weeks until the Wedding . . .*

Will arrived at Quincy's house early on the day he and the crew were supposed to go to Palm Springs for Jamal's bachelor party. Will had been to Quincy's home on many occasions. The spacious five-bedroom home was awe-inspiring. He rang the doorbell, and moments later, Karen opened the door.

"Hey, Will," Karen said.

"Hello, Mrs. Page." Will entered the house and made his way to the living room.

Will saw that Chantel and Quincy were already in the living room, and it did not take a smart man to figure out that something was up with the woman. Karen came into the living room and sat next to Chantel.

Even though Will had never been to jail before, he has been interrogated, and the experience was both eye-opening and rewarding. Will could discern when the detectives were fishing for evidence and when they had solid evidence. But Chantel and Karen were cold enough to scare the hardest criminal into a confession. They reminded him of the woman on that show called *The Closer*, except there were two of them.

"I know you're protected by this guy code, but come on. We won't say anything. We just wanted to know where you are going," Chantel said, without so much as a hi.

"I'm being straight with you. I don't know. I'm just along for the ride." Quincy said

"Uh-huh. There better not be any strippers there, you hear me?" Karen pointed a finger at Will.

Will felt the pressure of the women's statements.

"You know what the Bible says about strippers?" Karen asked.

"I don't know what the Bible says about strippers, but I do know that the Bible speaks against immodest behavior," Will told her.

"You just better keep that in mind when you're out. I love my husband, and God has brought him a mighty long ways." Karen paused and looked around to make sure that Quincy was not in earshot. "Keep him away from alcohol and casinos."

"You don't have to worry about that. I got you," Will said. He knew his brother was trying to walk the right path, but life had a way of throwing him a curveball. Finding out that his baby girl was pregnant would make any concerned father stray away from the path.

Jamal took in the desert air. It provided no reprieve for Jamal and his boys. Even in the middle of December, Palm Springs boasted warm temperatures. Quincy had booked a suite at the same hotel he and Karen had planned to stay at, until Sasha came home with her bad news. So Quincy had rescheduled, thinking that it was the perfect place for Jamal's bachelor party.

Jamal was nervous about his wedding being less than two weeks away. He and Chantel had decided to bring in the New Year as husband and wife. Everything would change after New Year's Eve, but for now, Jamal was going to enjoy his last trip with his close friends as a single man. He was also going to enjoy the bikini-clad women who hung out around the pool.

"This is the life, Q," Jamal said as he reclined in his beach chair.

Jamal had noticed that Quincy was quiet on the drive up to Palms Springs. He knew that the whole situation with Sasha had taken a toll, but now it seemed as if something else plagued him.

"You all right, Q?" Jamal asked.

"Oh yeah, I'm good," Quincy said, but Jamal believed differently.

"Man, it's a trip, because it wasn't until I became a Christian that I started traveling," Will interjected.

"Well, I'm just glad that we didn't go to Sin City," Chauncey added.

"Just be glad that you got invited," Quincy said as he sipped his iced tea.

# Chapter Thirty-six

## *Will*

Will waited for his brothers in the casino near the Parker Hotel. Quincy had raved about the restaurants at this casino and wanted the guys to get together and have dinner after playing a round of golf. After lunch at the swimming pool, the guys had decided to go play golf. Will had respectfully declined. The casinos in Palm Springs were not like the casinos in Los Angeles. Will pondered how the casinos in Palm Springs were situated in an affluent area, while the casinos in the inner cities were surrounded by poverty and decay. Will sat on a chair in the casino lobby and watched people with money walk in and out without a care in the world. He guessed that these people could afford to lose, while people who lived in Compton or Gardena couldn't afford to lose.

Will was not much of a party person. He was happy for his brother Jamal, who was getting married and had found the woman that he would always love. Even though Will did not classify himself as a romantic, he did marvel at the fact that two imperfect people could form a perfect union together. Maybe that was God's divine joke, Will thought as he removed his iPod from his front pocket and unrolled the headphones. He turned it on and decided to listen to his artist of the moment: Sam Cooke. Will could not recall where he was, but he heard a song called "A Change Is Gonna Come" on the day of the presidential election, and it was like Will's mini biography. The difference lay in the fact that Will knew a change had already occurred for him and that changes would continue to occur.

Will allowed Sam Cooke to serenade him, and he rested his forehead on his clasped hands. Usually, his mind raced through the different worries that made up his life. As the slow melody played, Will's thoughts played in slow rotation. His brother had been headed down the wrong path but had recently turned his life around. His father had not changed, his mother was too high to do anything, and his former gang was out for him.

He felt a gentle finger tap his knee, and when he looked up, a pretty, light-skinned girl with almond-shaped eyes smiled at him. Will knew that Sam Cooke would understand if he put him on pause to have a conversation with the girl.

"What are you listening to?"

"Sam Cooke, 'A Change Is Gonna Come.'"

"What you know about Sam Cooke?" the girl asked.

"Not much, but I know his song is about redemption, and I know that no man is beyond redemption and that every man needs to be redeemed."

"Oh, so you're one of those deep thinkers?" the girl asked.

"Not even. I'm just trying to be more conscious of my decisions."

"I'm Cherese." The girl extended her hand for a handshake.

Will told her his name, shook her hand, and sat back in his seat. Will didn't care too much for makeup. He felt like most women put too much on. Cherese, however, had just enough makeup to highlight her mocha complexion. She looked like a black Barbie doll. Flaw-less.

"You got a favorite verse?" Cherese asked as she pointed to Will's iPod.

"I love the whole song," Will replied.

"Okay, okay, tell me about it."

"I don't know. I guess you could hear the song and get down about your situation. But I listen and think about how one of the most powerful things that can happen in our lives is change. God gave me an opportunity to change, and I ain't wasting that gift on nobody."

"You're a Christian?" Cherese asked.

"To the fullest."

Cherese received a text message. "Hold on," she told Will. She responded to the text, and without looking up, she said, "I'm supposed to be meeting with my girl-friends. We're having this bridal shower for my best friend."

"That's crazy. I'm here for my best friend's bachelor party."

"Why are you not up in a strip club somewhere or a hotel room, making it rain?"

"Not my thing. I'd rather win a girl's heart with my mind than with my money."

"Hey! Now, that's what I'm talking about. It's rare to find a guy like you."

"I don't think so. I just do me, that's all," Will said.

Cherese let out a smile. She had a perfect set of white teeth, and her smile was complete with dimples. She was not a regular girl, the kind he came across in his neck of the woods.

"I got to get back to the party, but it was nice meeting you, Will. Maybe we could get together for coffee and talk about the Bible some more. What's your cell phone number?"

"For sure."

Will and Cherese exchanged phone numbers. Will shook her hand, and it felt both cold and soft. Cherese left, but her mango scent remained. Just then Will saw Chauncey and Jamal approaching him.

"Will, we got to find Q. He's missing," Jamal said.


Quincy savored the sweet taste of sin and noted how it offered pleasure and even made his skin come alive. He was using alcohol to drown out his problems, but in the back of his mind he knew that come morning, he would regret his actions. Still, Quincy rolled the dice and let it ride.

"Come on, six. You're overdue."

Quincy rolled a six, and the people that surrounded the table exploded in cheers. Quincy took another swig as a sign of his victory. He picked up the dice and rolled again without hesitation. This time he was not a winner, but he was unfazed by the deep sighs of the people who had just lost by betting on him. Quincy took a swig, and it was no different than what he felt when he won. He kept on gambling, throwing both the dice and caution to the wind. He just did not care. It wasn't until the ninth roll of the dice that his conscience rolled in, in the form of his two brothers Will, Chauncey and Jamal.

"Q, man, what are you doing?" Jamal asked.

"Just having a little fun. Shouldn't you be back at the hotel with some Luke dancers?" Quincy rolled the dice, and the crowd roared.

"You haven't been drinking, have you?" Will asked.

"No. This is primarily iced tea." Quincy held up his drink.

"Come on, man. Don't go down this road. I know you're going through it, we all are, but let's just go," Jamal said.

"If I roll a seven, I'll pay for your and Chantel's honeymoon. Wherever you want to go," Quincy said as he shook the dice.

"Come on, seven," Jamal said, and he was nudged by Will.

Quincy rolled an eight, and that loss stung him. He lost twenty grand, which was one man's life savings and another man's salary. For Quincy, it was the equivalent of a speeding ticket. With that, he did what he should have done a long time ago, and that was fold. Quincy left, his brothers escorting him out of the casino. Once outside, Will and Jamal stood him up against the wall.

"Q, what's wrong with you? Don't let your daughter cause you to trip like this," Jamal said.

"Sasha cheated on Dwight, and she's not sure if he is the father," Quincy said after a long, awkward moment.

"Wow!" Jamal said. "Q, you've got to stop punishing yourself for the things that your daughter did."

"I've never failed at anything, and to fail at parenting is a bitter pill to swallow." Quincy knew he had disappointed his brothers, but there was someone who he held to a greater standard that he had let down. "Father, forgive me for my sins. I just don't know what to do."

Quincy's prayer did not go unnoticed, and he appreciated that his brothers carried him to the car and did not interrupt his prayer with his Father.

# Chapter Thirty-seven

## *Will*

Will took Joshua to lunch and brought him back to his parents' place. For a week, Will had spent as much time as he could going through the scriptures with Joshua and helping him with his homework. Not once did Will's mother reach out to talk to her son. Will found this odd, but not surprising. She knew that Joshua was with Will. Will figured his mother knew that Joshua was safe. Will wanted his brother to have some foundation before he headed home. The scriptures said that a person should work out their salvation, and Will wanted to help his brother in that cause.

The motorcycle was too dangerous for Joshua to ride on the back of, so Will took the bus with his brother back to their apartment on Atlantic. As they walked up to the apartment, Will felt uneasiness set in. Something was wrong, and Will started to look in the different corners around the apartment building, which were dark even in the daytime. He waited for an ambush, while at the same time he did not break his stride.

"You all right, bro?" Joshua asked.

"Yeah." Will told a lie because he did not want his brother to freak out. Will was not sure why he felt uncomfortable, but he knew that he could not dismiss a feeling as persuasive as the one going on in his stomach.

They ascended the stairs, and Will's uneasiness only grew. When they arrived at the apartment, the key did not work in the door. Will peeked in a window. The apartment looked empty as far as tenants went, but it still had a lot of furniture. Will took a closer look and noticed all the lights were out. For as long as Will could remember, Carroll had barely left the house. No one being home was beyond peculiar.

"Look!" Joshua pointed to the sign on the door.

Will didn't know how he had missed the sign. He figured that he did not want to accept the truth that the apartment had been vacated. A notice of eviction was posted on the front door of their parents' apartment. Will's uneasiness turned into a cold chill that spread through his body. He did not know where his parents were, and he didn't know where his baby sister was, either.

"Let's roll, Josh." Will tapped his brother on the chest, and as they turned to head downstairs, he saw a dozen members of the Untouchables gang.

"I got this, bro." Josh headed downstairs.

Will did not know if he was going to make it to find his mother and sister, so he did what he knew how to do best. *Father, protect me and Josh, and allow us to find our family. Devil, you have no authority, and I know that with God all things are possible.*

"What up, J-Rock?" asked Curtis, who had taken over the gang from D-Loc, as Will finished his prayer.

"What up, man?" Josh had reached the bottom of the steps.

When Will made it downstairs and stood next to Joshua, all he got was a smirk from Curtis.

"What up, Will?" Curtis asked.

"Nothing much," Will replied. Even now Will could take Curtis in a fight, but wisdom had to prevail.

"That's burnt how you did the fam. Some think that you're responsible for getting D-Loc killed," Curtis said.

"You know I ain't had nothing to do with that. D-Loc got his own self killed." Will's tone was a bit more aggressive than he wanted it to be.

"What, cuz?" Curtis reached for his .45 pistol, which he had tucked underneath his shirt.

Will wished that somehow God could remove him and Joshua from this situation, because Will was certain he was about to die. He didn't mind dying while standing on his two feet for something he believed in, but he didn't want any harm to come to his brother.

"It's cool. Curtis, it's cool." Josh stood between Will and Curtis.

Will moved Josh out of the way and stood his ground. There existed nothing but space and opportunity between Curtis and Will.

"Naw, it ain't cool. He better be lucky that you're a part of the set, otherwise I'd murk him right now." Curtis brandished his weapon.

Will wanted to snatch the gun from Curtis and empty the clip. He felt horrible that he was still having those thoughts. The devil was playing with his mind, and the devil was whispering thoughts of a coward and a punk.

"My brother is no longer a part of the set. He's given his life to the Lord," Will said.

"What he talking about, J?" Curtis asked, furious.

"I did. I want out," Josh said timidly.

"Well, you both about to meet the Lord." Curtis raised his gun and aimed toward Will's face.

Will had had enough of people who felt like they could put a gun in his face. Will snatched hold of Curtis's wrist and turned the gun on Curtis and rested the muzzle underneath his chin. More guns were drawn at this point, but none were fired. Will looked into Curtis's eyes and saw a scared little boy, for Curtis had started to whimper and cry.

"You guys don't have to be a part of a gang to be strong," Will said to anyone within earshot. "I'm stronger now than I've ever been, and all I had to do was embrace love, forgiveness, and faith." Will let go of Curtis, but he did not let go of the gun.

"I ask you guys to forgive me for walking away, but I felt like my life is worth more than taking from others. I believe you guys are meant for more as well." Will removed the clip and emptied the bullets from the chamber before laying the gun on the ground. "I just wish you guys could see yourselves the way God sees you."

A squad car passed by and stopped in the middle of the street. Members of the gang started to disperse to avoid being harassed. Will was grateful for the boys in blue. Curtis left with his pride severely damaged. Will waited for the squad car to leave before he wiped down the gun with his T-shirt and disposed of it in a nearby Dumpster.

"Josh, take one good last look at this apartment, because we're never coming back here."


Long Beach was all Will's mother knew. They had moved to different parts of the city, from North Long Beach, by Jordan High School, to a few blocks away from Long Beach Poly. Of all the places, Will remembered when they lived downtown, next to the beach. His mother never took him to the beach for fear that Will might drown. Funny how she had shielded him from one danger but had left him vulnerable to many other dangers in the world. No matter the circumstances, Will knew that his mother would never leave Long Beach. For Will, that fact alone was good enough.

In the middle of his living room, while Joshua played his Xbox 360, Will sat with his eyes closed and searched for his mother in his mind. He searched for places he remembered his mom taking him to. Most of the images were fragmented, and after a few minutes, frustration set in.

*Lord, help me to find my family. Lord, please!* Will prayed and meditated some more, but to no avail. Will felt like his prayers were useless, until an image of a house popped into his mind, a brown house that barely held together. Will focused in on this image, and another piece came to him. Will remembered a rusty, crooked gate that he had to enter, along with a broken screen door. Will tried to settle his mind and not get too excited, lest he lose both the image and its relevance to his current search for his mother and sister.

Will concentrated more, and he remembered playing on the floor with some kid and his mother lying on the couch, high on drugs. Will's mind went back to the house, and he tried to remember anything about the surroundings. That was when he remembered that the house was near a freeway, and knew where his mother could possibly be.

"Josh," Will said as he opened his eyes.

"Yeah?"

"Stay here until I get back. You understand?" Will said.

"Uh-huh." Joshua continued to play the game.

Will walked over to Jamal's room and knocked on the door.

"What's going on?" Jamal said as he opened the door.

"I need to borrow your car!" Will told him.

"You're tripping," Jamal said.

"I think I know where my mom and sister are, and if so, I can't get them here on a bike."

Jamal grumbled at Will's request, which was understandable. Jamal had poured a lot of money into that new car and would not want to see anything happen to it.

"You owe me big for this one," Jamal said before he turned his back to Will and snatched the keys off of his dresser. "You need me to go with you?"

"Naw, I'm cool. If you can just keep an eye on Josh, I'd appreciate it," Will said.

Jamal gave Will a head nod in agreement, and Will shot out of the house and made his way to the elevator that led to the underground parking lot. The short elevator ride could not prevent Will's mind from drifting to the what-ifs. What if his mom was not there? What if his mom had OD'd on drugs? What if Elisha had been hurt in the process? What-ifs could drive a man over the edge, so Will focused first on getting out of the elevator and then on getting to Artesia Street, which was where the house was located, as fast as possible.

Once Will entered the parking lot, he did not have any trouble spotting Jamal's Camaro. The sound the engine made when Will turned on the ignition let the driver know that this car was not built for an amateur. Will was not an amateur, and his past as a car thief proved that he could handle a car. If he found himself in a tight spot, he had the tools to maneuver out of it with the right kind of car. Will sped out of the parking lot and raced along Long Beach Boulevard. It was a long shot that his mother was at the house in Will's vision. It was a chance he was willing to take, though.

The house Will used to go to with his mother when he was a kid could've been a crack house or a friend's house. So long as his mother and sister were there,

Will couldn't care less. It took Will about ten minutes to get to Artesia, and when he reached the street, he made a sharp left toward the area where the 710 and the 91 crossed. Will had just got past the freeways when he saw a liquor store and a small neighborhood to the right. He made a right turn, and at the end of the block was the brown house he had envisioned.

It would've been a shame if Will had used his mind to tap into forgotten memories and pull forth an image of a hot spot for his mom, only for his mom not to be there. Will parked the car along the side of the street facing the house. The house was at a dead end, so Will would have to do a U-turn to get out. As he approached the house, Will could tell that it had once been a luxurious two-story. Now it would be a prime location for inner-city dramas and horror films.

Will arrived at the door and gave a solid knock, which might have been misinterpreted as coming from the police. Will heard rumbling and the sound of things being rearranged.

"Who is it?" a woman yelled from the other side of the door.

"It's Will, Carroll's son."

More rumbling ensued before the door opened and a heavy woman with gap teeth smiled at Will. "My, my, you've turned into one fine young man. You don't remember me, do you? I'm your Auntie Pat."

"I'm sorry I don't." What Will did remember was that he didn't have an auntie named Pat. "Is my mother here?"

The woman didn't answer. She just opened the door wider and extended her hand for Will to come in. Will had thought his parents' house was foul-smelling, but their house didn't have anything on this place. He entered the living room, and there was his mother, in the same position as in his memories, on the couch, high.

"Hey, baby," his mom said with her eyes half closed.

"Mom, where's Elisha?"

"She's running around here somewhere." She pointed lazily in a random direction.

"She's in the back room, just past the stairs." The heavyset woman pointed Will in the right direction.

Will made his way toward the back room, and along the way, he passed a couple that had forgotten to close the door before they got into having sex. The smell grew worse as Will reached the back room, where his sister was. Will opened the door and nearly tripped over the numerous toys on the floor, and there was his sister, Elisha, asleep. Peaceful. He didn't want to wake her, but he didn't want her to stay in that house any longer. He grabbed Elisha in his arms and walked out of the room and made his way back toward the living room.

"Mom, we're getting out of here. Where's Elisha's car seat?"

All Carroll did was laugh and rub her nose.

"Mom!"

"What do I need with a car seat? I ain't got no car. I ain't got no home, neither. I needed the money," Carroll mumbled.

"Them crackers put her out and didn't care that she had a family," the heavyset woman said.

Will could not put his baby sister's life at risk. If he was caught driving an infant without a car seat, then he would go to jail and the car would be impounded.

"I have a car seat," the heavyset woman said.

"Could I borrow it? I'm taking them home with me."

The heavyset woman went upstairs, and Will switched the arm he held Elisha with and used his free hand to grab his mother by the arm.

"Let go of me!" Carroll said, stumbling around, trying to free herself.

"Mom, we're going home, and that's it!"

Will would have to make two trips due to the limited space the Camaro offered. Elisha was his top priority, so Will proceeded to install the car seat in the passenger's seat His mother stood on the sidewalk, barely able to stand. Will prayed that his mother would be there when he got back, but for right now he had to think about his sister.


Will knew that when Quincy let him stay at the condo, the condition was that the family drama did not follow him. Will broke that promise today, as his mother lay on the couch, oblivious to what was going on in the world around her. Elisha walked around the apartment, getting into all kinds of mischief, which Joshua had to clean up.

"Mom," Will called and gave her a firm shake.

"What? What?" Carroll opened her eyes and looked around the room. "Who are these guys?"

"This is Jamal—Will pointed—"my best friend, and this is Pastor Dawkins, my pastor."

"Hello, ma'am. Your son called me over," Titus said.

"Mom, I want you to get some help, and Pastor has a program that can help you get clean."

"I don't need no help," Carroll snapped.

"Mom, it's time."

Will believed that the word *time* was one of the most powerful words in the English language. Time was the one thing that Will was certain that everyone would run out of! Will regretted how he had used his time for the first part of his life, but he remained convinced that he would make good use of the time he had left.

The front door closed, and Will recognized the sound of quality dress shoes as they tapped on the marble floor. Quincy entered the living room in his custom-made suit, minus a tie.

"What's going on here?" Quincy said.

Will's eyes stayed locked on Quincy's eyes as Quincy acknowledged everyone in the room. "Q, can I talk to you in private?" Will asked.

"Let's go into the office." Quincy headed to his former office, which was located in the room next to the front door.

Will followed Quincy to his office, and if the way a man walked was any indication of his disposition, then Will knew that his friend was beyond furious. Will entered the office, where Quincy had already assumed a position in the middle of the floor, with his hands on his hips and a look of disbelief on his face. Will closed the door to muffle their conversation.

"What the heck is going on?" Quincy asked.

"My mother and baby sister got evicted from their place. I found her at some crack house with my sister on the north side."

Will could tell his statement hit Quincy like a punch in the gut. The last thing Will wanted was to be at odds with his friend, but God had made it clear in both Will's mind and heart that he should go and get his family.

"Whew. That's rough for your baby sister. So what are you going to do?"

"I don't know." Will shrugged his shoulders.

"Well, you better figure it out, because you know our deal."

"That's my family, Q. I just can't leave them out in the cold. You know that!"

"Your mother is a grown woman, and she has made her choices. Part of the problem is that no one has held her accountable for anything," Quincy said.

Will had never proclaimed his mother to be a saint, but Quincy had no right to talk about her like she was trash.

"That's my mother, Q. What's the point of being a Christian if I can't even help my own family?"

"The point is you realize that you can't even save yourself, let alone anyone else," Quincy said.

"I appreciate everything you have done for me, and I love you like a father figure," Will replied.

"Hey, hey! I'm already feeling old enough these days." Quincy scratched his goatee. "I know this is your mother, but for too long your family has held you down and has made poor choices, which set you and your brother on the wrong path."

"I know, but God had a plan and a path, and I now understand more than anything that God does not want me to abandon my family."

"So what are you going to do?" Quincy asked.

"I'm going to get her help. Enroll her in a program and see what happens," Will said.

"Are you prepared to face the challenges if you do all of this and it doesn't work?"

The knock on the door was subtle enough to be overlooked if it weren't for the fact that Will and Quincy had stopped talking. Will opened the door, and his mother was on the other side.

"I'm sorry, but I have to say something," Carroll said

"No, you don't, Mom. Just go back into the living room, and I'll be there in a second."

"No, I'm not. I'm your mother, and though I haven't been much of a mother to you, I'm going to say something," Carroll replied in a sharp tone.

Will's stomach turned, because his mother had never been aggressive and Quincy never minced words.

"I appreciate all that you've done for my son, and I know that you didn't have to do any of it," Carroll began.

"Will is a good kid, and he loves you dearly. I hope you know that," Quincy replied.

"He is." Carroll shifted her eyes from Quincy to the floor.

"Mom, I love you, and I'm going to get you help. The church has this program, and you don't have to pay anything for the program, and we will provide for you everything that you need to be delivered."

Carroll didn't say anything. She just wiped a solitary tear from her face. Will knew that his mother was moved by hearing words she had not heard in a long time: "I love you!"

# Chapter Thirty-eight

## *Jamal*

*One Week until the Wedding . . .*

Lately, Jamal had been reading all the Bible verses that related to courage. He had discovered that courage was the ability to carry out an action with confidence in spite of enormous obstacles. It took courage on both Chantel's and Jamal's part to walk up the driveway of the Atkinses' home. Jamir took Jamal by the hand and walked slightly ahead, while Jamal kept a tight grip on Chantel's hand.

"I'm nervous," Chantel said.

"So am I," Jamal replied.

"Poppa!" Jamir patted the front door.

Moments later Gerald Atkins opened the door, and his face did not reflect that he was happy to see Jamal and Chantel, but when he looked down, he lit up at the sight of Jamir.

"Hey, boy." Mr. Atkins picked up Jamir and squeezed him gently.

Jamir was the closest Mr. Atkins would ever come to being with his son Clay on this side of life. Jamal understood how important it was for Jamir to be in his grandfather's life and vice versa.

"Hey, Mr. Atkins. We were wondering if we could come in and talk," Jamal said.

Mr. Atkins did not respond. All he did was step aside and extended his hand. Jamal allowed Jamir to lead the way. The boy walked into the house and made a beeline to the den area, where some of his favorite toys resided. Brenda Atkins, Jamir's grandmother, was already in the living room, watching *Dr. Phil.*

"Hello, Mrs. Atkins," Jamal and Chantel said in off-key unison.

Brenda Atkins was equally as shocked as her husband had been upon first seeing the couple.

"Good afternoon. God bless you," Mrs. Atkins said.

Jamal and Chantel had a seat on the love seat, and when Mr. Atkins took a seat next to his wife on the couch, the room fell silent. Jamir played with the toy drum set his grandfather had bought him, which sat in the middle of the room. Jamir was the only thing that sustained a fragile line of connection between the two families.

"So what's up?" Mr. Atkins asked.

Jamal didn't know where to start. Between that night at the club where Jamal confessed that he had slept with Chantel while she was still with Clay, to this moment, there was no easy way to begin.

"Every time I come to pick Jamir up, I wonder if today is going to be the day when I finally come inside and have an overdue conversation about Clay," Jamal said, and he drew a blank stare from the Atkinses. "Clay and I were like brothers. No one took his death harder than me."

"I doubt that," Mr. Atkins said.

"I'm sorry. I didn't mean it that way." Jamal paused to try to gather himself after the poor choice of words. The tension was building. "There's not a day that passes when I don't wish that I had that moment back. I've made a lot of mistakes, but that is one mistake I wish I could have back."

The women started to wipe their eyes over the loss of Clay. Mrs. Atkins cried over the loss of a son. Chantel cried over the loss of a lover. Both men were locked in a tense stare down.

Jamal felt like he was trying to make an ice sculpture with a plastic knife. He searched for the right words that would convey his deepest sincerity and found his stream of consciousness quite shallow.

"I love him, and I didn't want to hurt him. But I can't deny my love for Chantel. Even though what we did was wrong and we betrayed someone we confessed to love, I'm learning to let go of the burden of Clay's death."

"This is what you wanted to come in and talk about?" Mr. Atkins asked. "You wanted to come into my living room and tell me that you don't feel responsible for Clay's death!"

"I'm not saying that!" Jamal replied.

"Then what *are* you saying, Jamal?" Mrs. Atkins asked.

"I'm saying that I'm not going to walk around feeling condemned for a mistake I made years ago. What I did was wrong, but Clay chose to respond by getting into that fight. I would've let him beat me up and be over with it."

"You knew that Clay was a hothead. Why on earth would you tell him at a club, of all places?" Mr. Atkins asked.

"I don't know what I was thinking. I just know that I couldn't lie to him anymore."

"He loved you," Mrs. Atkins said before she looked at a sobbing Chantel. "Both of you, and you two broke my son's heart."

"I loved your son, even though he didn't always treat me right," Chantel replied.

"So that makes what you did okay?" Ms. Atkins asked.

Jamir crossed the floor in between the battle lines and climbed under the love seat, next to Chantel. He had a toy in his hands, and Jamal was reminded that this was not about him and Chantel. This was about Jamir.

"If you feel so guilty, why haven't you said something before? Why now?" Mrs. Atkins asked.

"Because I was too scared to face you. I was so guilt ridden, and when I discovered that Jamir was not my biological son, that made matters even worse."

"You didn't call, and you didn't visit. We loved you like a son, and it was like we lost both of you at the same time," Mrs. Atkins said.

Jamal did not know that the Atkinses felt that way about him. A lot of families talked about loving and treating their friends like their family, but the Atkinses truly did see Jamal as a son and were hurt that he left them alone with their grief.

"I learned that guilt and condemnation are tools used by the devil to keep us from moving on with our lives. I loved Clay, and if the roles were reversed, I would be devastated, but I would still want Clay to be happy. I love Jamir like a son, and I will raise him to be a better man than me. Though Chantel and I were wrong for what we did, I love her more than any other woman on this planet, and I want to spend the rest of my life with both Chantel and Jamir. And I don't want you guys to hate me."

"We don't hate you. I just wish that Clay had been around long enough for you to influence him," Mr. Atkins said.

To say that Mr. Atkins's words threw Jamal off was an understatement. For years Jamal had walked in the shadow of the mighty Clay. Up until his death there was nothing that Jamal possessed that Clay envied.

"He was talking to me about how you had joined the church and had started to make a change. He even thought about possibly making a change as well. I really wanted to see what a changed Clay would look like," Mr. Atkins said.

Tears leaked out of Jamal's eyes without a forewarning. He would've loved for his best friend to give his life to the Lord. They would've been brothers in Christ. Shame covered Jamal's face, and he buried his face in his hands. He recognized the warm hand of Chantel rubbing his back and the small, cold hands of Jamir touching his hand. But the firm hand that Mr. Atkins placed on his shoulder lifted the weight that Jamal felt. Jamal lifted his head to find Mr. Atkins with tears in his eyes.

"I think we all have been living in the past, and with this little one right here—Mr. Atkins pointed at Jamir—"we need to come together as a family and raise him, because I know that's what my son would've wanted."

"I'm so sorry," Jamal said.

Gerald didn't response in words, but in actions. He gave Jamal a hug, and Mrs. Atkins joined in and gave them all a hug. For the first time in years, joy permeated both the Atkinses' home and everyone's hearts.

# Chapter Thirty-nine

## *Titus*

This was the first time Titus would be traveling with his wife, Grace. This would be Grace's first trip to Atlanta, and Titus wanted to make the trip special. He did not know how his wife would handle traveling with him. Titus was aware of the change in seasons. Takeout had been replaced with full-course meals. A cold bed with extra space was now warm and occupied. Whenever Titus traveled with his relatively young staff, he would enjoy their youthful lifestyle. They would live out of suitcases, stay up virtually all night, and then live off of their caffeine drug of choice.

"Are you nervous, babe?" Grace said as she emerged from the bathroom in a cotton candy nightgown.

"No. I don't know why, but this year feels different. It feels like the men are hungry for change."

"Well, that's God, and I know God will put on your heart what to say to them." Grace made her way to Titus's side of the closet.

Out of his peripheral vision, he saw Grace open his side of the closet, which was organized military style, with his suits on the top rack and his shoes, still in their boxes, on the bottom. She removed his Italian black cotton suit and laid it across the bed.

"Now, how did you know I was going to pick that?"

"You usually wear black when you travel, and you look good in this suit," Grace said as she found a crimson tie and laid it with the suit. She then laid a garment bag next to the suit and tie, placed them inside the bag, and then zipped it up. Grace hung the suit back on the rack.

Next, she made her way to Titus's dresser, where he had methodically laid out everything, from his watch to his wallet. She continued to pack Titus's overnight bag, which was already half full.

"You're an awesome woman."

"Why you say that?" Grace shrugged as she tossed a pair of black dress socks into the bag.

"Because you take good care of me."

"You take good care of your congregation. Besides, you needed it."

"I was doing okay on my own." Titus swaggered over to Grace.

"Yeah, but something was missing, and it takes a good woman to see that!"

# Chapter Forty

## *Quincy*

Quincy and Karen decided to take Sasha back to her apartment in Berkeley. The drive up was solemn, to say the least. There was not much conversation, except for where to stop to get gas and food. Quincy wanted to make sure that his baby girl and future grandchild made it back safely. He had spent a lot of money so that Sasha could have her own apartment. It was part of his distraction-proof plan, to give her every and any advantage she needed. He knew that this semester would be a wash for Sasha as far as grades went, but he hoped that she could find a way to get back into school. He just needed to adjust his approach.

"Mom, Dad, I have something to tell you," As they stood in her apartment.Sasha said.

"Baby, I don't think your father and I can handle any more confessions," Karen said.

"Yeah, this isn't an Usher song," Quincy replied.

"I know I've disappointed you guys, but I have to tell you that it wasn't the separation that caused me to spin out of control."

"Oh really? What was it, then?" Quincy asked.

"I just felt like I had no control of my life. You guys have set this standard that made me feel like I had to be perfect, and when I got on my own, I just wanted to loosen up and have fun."

"You didn't have to be perfect. You just had to be responsible. Your father and I have always wanted what was best for you."

"Look, people make mistakes, and this right here is a hot mess," Quincy said. "I'm not going to even lie to you, but you have to remember that everything in life comes with a cost. If you want to be brilliant, it may cost you not being able to have fun most of the time. If you want to have fun, it may cost you reaching your full potential. You have to decide what you want for your life."

"I know, and I know that God will help me to get my life back on track," Sasha said.

That was the first time Quincy had even heard Sasha mention God. He realized that God was much more skilled at redemption than he himself was.

"Listen, Sasha, your mother and I have been talking, and we want you to come back home."

Sasha smiled.

"Before you get all excited, this will not be a picnic," Quincy added. "You understand me? You're going to have to be accountable and be a responsible parent."

"Of course, Dad."

Quincy headed toward the window next to where Sasha's bed use to be to view the cherry blossoms that covered the sidewalks in abundance at Berkeley. "We both want to see you be a good mother, which we know you are more than capable of, but we don't want you to give up on school and a career. You and your child are both going to need it. So if you want, you can move back home, enroll at UCLA or USC, it doesn't matter which, and we will hire a nanny to watch the baby while you're at school. But once you're finished with class and studying, then you are going to be with your child. Partying is over for you until you get back on your feet."

"Okay, Dad, I will do it. I'll go back to school."

Quincy looked outside the window again and saw a familiar face.

"I'll be right back," Quincy said as he headed toward the door.

"But, Dad, we have a reservation for lunch."

Quincy did not respond; he just headed out the door.

"Dwight!" Quincy said.

Dwight stopped and turned around. He had on a polo shirt and a pair of Dockers, the complete opposite of what he wore the last time Quincy saw him. Quincy had not heard anything from Dwight for a while, and he'd wondered what he had been up to.

"Hey. What's going on, Mr. Page?"

"Nothing much. What's going on with you?"

"Just on my way to school."

"School." Quincy nearly choke on his own word.

"Yeah, I enrolled at Santa Rosa Junior College. I'm trying to get my GE courses out of the way."

"So what's with the clothes?"

"I'm trying to dress like the man that I want to be." Dwight spoke with a lot of pride.

Quincy was blown away by how much Dwight had matured in such a short time span.

"Mr. Page, I never got a chance to thank you for taking me to the men's retreat. I've been reading my Bible since and trying to find a church home."

Quincy hated how things had turned out between Dwight and Sasha. Sasha had no way of contacting the other potential father, and the pending paternity test after the baby was born made Quincy sick to his stomach. "I apologize for how everything turned out between you and Sasha, but God has a plan for your life, and I can see it. I'm going to tell you something that my father once told me. Few men make their mistake going toward God. Their mistake usually comes from trying to go away from God."

Dwight put his head down and bit his bottom lip. The situation with Sasha was still a very sore one for Dwight. "Thanks, Mr. Page, and I plan to be there when the baby is born."

"I believe you," Quincy said.

The two exchanged handshakes and went about their way. Quincy was moved by the power that the Holy Spirit could produce.

# Chapter Forty-one

## *Will*

Will did not like hospitals. He could not find comfort in a place that housed the sick. From the cool temperature, the white walls, and the people walking around in their pajamas, Will had an eerie feeling. But since he became a Christian, he'd realized that church was a lot like a hospital that housed the sick and the afflicted, and like a hospital, the church was designed for recovery, deliverance, and salvation.

It was like Will was looking at his mother for the first time. For years he had avoided eye contact, because he did not want to behold the junkie that had birthed him. If someone asked Will to describe his mother, Will's description would stop at "brown skin and black hair." He wouldn't be able to describe his mother's eyes, because he had never looked long enough to tell what color they were. Will also wouldn't be able to tell them about his mother's smile, because he never saw her smile until he went to visit her at Promises Recovery Center, a recovery center that worked in partnership with Will's church.

Will had read somewhere that it took twenty-eight days to break a habit. Well, Will believed that his mother was halfway through, and she had never looked better. Sure, her face had wrinkles and scars as a result of a hard lifestyle, but when she smiled, Will was moved to tears, because he was reminded that no matter how much the devil tried to tear a person down, through faith a person could rise from the ashes.

"You look great, Mom," Will said.

The sun baked their necks, while the wind tickled their skin. The sky was a calming blue, and Will sat there without a worry in the world.

"I can't thank you enough, son. I was in a dark place for so long, and then it was like God shined a light and the darkness scattered." Carroll got teary-eyed and wiped her eyes.

"No man can do what God has done in both of our lives. He has a purpose for both of us," Will said.

"I know that's true. He kept me."

Will felt the kind of love that would cause him to stand in harm's way. While his mother was in recovery for drug abuse, Will was in recovery from toxic anger, which had almost exploded within him.

"Have you talked to Dad?" Will asked.

"Yeah, he called and told me that he was working on something that would get us in a new place."

"And what did you tell him?"

"I told him that I didn't want to have anything to do with that lifestyle."

Will started to think of the possibilities of where his father could be. Will knew his father was going to go for a big score, but where? Will forgot about his mother being right in front of him as he contemplated his father's whereabouts. Will decided to think back to all the times his father got caught. Every time his father got released from prison, he would go back to the spot where he got caught and rob it again, this time with success. It was like Odell spent his whole prison term figuring out where he went wrong and correcting his mistakes. Will wished Odell had the same resolve with his family.

That meant that Odell was headed to one place, and it was a risk, but Will had to try. Odell's ego had been damaged, and for that he was willing to risk anything to restore his honor. Time was not a luxury for Will, and he had to find his father before he made a mistake that he would spend the rest of his life regretting.

"Listen, Mom, you stay strong, and let me know if you need anything."

"Where are you going?" Carroll asked.

"I think you know where," Will said with a slight smile.

"I'm proud of you, son."

"So am I! I love you!"

"Oh God, I love you too, and I thank God for you!" Carroll wiped the tears from her eyes.

Will left his mom, thinking of how powerful God's love was if it could restore his family. He just had one more piece left in the puzzle.

Odell being so predictable had its benefits. Will knew that if his father was going to make a big score, then it was going to be a European used car lot in Signal Hill. This car lot was owned by a rich Armenian who loved European cars to the point where he had a car lot full of used BMWs, Mercedes, Porsches, and so on. This was the same car lot that Odell had been pinched for stealing from before. Maybe Will's father thought that the second time would be a charm.

Will approached the car lot with his eyes wide open and his senses running at an all-time high. He couldn't afford to get caught trying to help his father. The Armenian had some of the most expensive cars in the country. His security was formidable but not impenetrable.

The gate had been taken out with a bolt cutter. Will slid his small frame through the gate and noticed that the surveillance camera had also been taken out, which meant he had only a few minutes before someone from security would arrive. Will scurried through the car lot in search of his father. Will could predict any move his father would make, except which car he planned to take.

The sound of a siren caused Will to duck down behind a Mercedes C-Class sedan. He hoped that his heartbeat did not give away his position. Luckily for Will, the siren was for some other matter in the area. Time continued to work against Will. He waited a few more seconds before he resumed his search for his father. Will had scurried across a few more rows of cars when he rolled up on his father, who was trying to steal an Audi A4.

"Dad, don't do this!" Will tried to whisper.

"Get out of here!" Odell waved him on and kept working.

"No, you're not about to ruin your life. That would be your third strike!"

"I ain't got time for one of your family moments," Odell said as he popped open the door of the Audi.

"Can you give the system another twenty-five years of your life? Is it worth it?" Will's words managed to stop Odell's progress.

"This is all I know," Odell said, contorting his face to fight back the tears.

"You know it's not. You know your family loves you and desperately wants for us to be a family for once in this life. To not worry about the police busting down our door. Come on, Dad. Don't do this. Just have a talk with your son instead."

Sirens could be heard in the distance, and Will realized that he was out of time. "It's time to make a decision, and you know what's the right thing to do."

Odell hesitated, and then he banged his fist on the hood of the car before he closed the door and picked up his tools.

"Dad, there's no time!" Will took Odell by the arm and ran toward the front entrance, and his father followed right along with him. Will got through the gate with ease, but when he turned back, Odell ran back inside the car lot.

"Dad, there's no time!" Will yelled again as the sirens got closer.

There was no response, and it was decision time. Will ran back inside the car lot against his better judgment. He ran right to the Audi his father had tried to steal and discovered that his father had left his tool kit.

"Let's go!" Will took his father by the arm, but Odell fought him off.

"I'm through running, son. Go on without me."

Will said nothing. He let his actions do all the talking. Will resolved in his mind that he was not going to leave without his father. Will took his father by the arm again and led him to a corner of the car lot that also had a gate. Will took the bolt cutter and cut open the lock. He slid the gate open wide enough for him and his father to get out just as a squad car came to a halt.

The two made it around the corner before they heard the police sirens. There was no way that Odell would've escaped on his own, and Will knew that he had just saved his father from a life in the penitentiary.

"That was a close one," Odell said, out of breath.

"I know, but this is the last time you run. You understand?" Will asked.

Odell gave Will a head nod, and they made their way to a diner two blocks away from the car dealership.

"Let's go in here and chill until things die down," Will said as he opened the door for his father. Odell entered the restaurant, and Will followed behind him.

"You can have a seat anywhere," the hostess said, pointing to an open area.

Will and Odell had a seat at a table with two chairs in the back. Odell hid his tool kit underneath the table. The hostess handed them menus, and Will sat his down in front of him, while Odell thumbed through his.

"Why would you try to rob the place that got you pinched the last time?" Will shrugged his shoulders in confusion.

"Needed to make a play. That car would've had me and your mother set."

"You wouldn't have made it. You realized that it was too short of a window for you to make it."

"I could've." Odell looked at Will for a moment before he shook his head. "Maybe you're right, but how did you know?"

"You also like to boost cars after midnight, when it's late. You wanted to steal from this lot out of pride, since it beat you the first time around."

"Look at my son. He knows his old man." Odell cracked a smile.

"I know the car thief. I want to know my father before he started boosting cars."

"Shoot, I've been doing that for so long, I couldn't tell you what I was like."

"I know guys who will slug it out with the police before they go to prison. Why do you risk your freedom?" Will asked.

"Because that's the only time I feel free. I steal a car, and I might cruise to Vegas or Phoenix. Heck, I even went to Washington one time. Man, I loved it. Then it was like I was on a leash. I'll get snapped right back to the reality that I have a family and kids, and you know . . . I got to go back."

"I'm surprised you didn't stay gone," Will said.

"I thought about it on more than one occasion."

"But?"

"But that's just it. What if I was killed in a crash or took a bullet? I mean, if I'm around, I can at least count on four people being at my funeral to send me off. If I die out there in the middle of nowhere, I would be a John Doe."

Will used to have that same fear of dying and no one he loved being around. He didn't want to be born Will and die John.

"Then it's time to start new."

"I'm too old to start over, son. Maybe that's why I resented you so much. You were able to hit pause on where your life was headed and start over with this religion thing."

"What can I get for you, gentlemen?" the waitress asked.

"The number three special. Eggs scrambled," Will said and handed the waitress his menu without looking at her.

"T-bone steak and eggs. I want my steak medium well, and he's paying," said Odell. Both the waitress and Will let out a smirk before the waitress left.

Will continued the conversation. "Men throughout the Bible made a drastic change in their lives. Moses, Abraham, even Paul."

"We're not living in the Bible times," Odell said.

"God's word is still true. You can change. You're still alive. Every moment you live is a chance at redemption."

"Who's going to hire a middle-aged ex-con?"

"The Salvation Army! I put in a good word for you. They're looking for truck drivers. The pay isn't all that great, but it's honest work."

"Where am I going to stay?"

"We'll work on that together, but you have to be willing to put this life in your rearview."

Moments later, the waitress appeared with two hot plates of food. She placed them on the table, and Will bent his head to pray.

"Heavenly Father—" Will began, but he felt someone grab his hand. He looked up to see his father with his head bowed. "Thank you, Jesus!"

# Chapter Forty-two

## Jamal

### *New Year's Eve / Wedding Day*

Jamal preferred Italian-cut suits to penguin suits. He had deviated from the traditional tuxedo, and his best men had followed suit. His black tailor-cut suit was accentuated by a purple tie and matching handkerchief. A purple scarf was draped around his shoulders, and the transformation was complete. Jamal was hesitant to wear purple. He preferred a color that was more masculine; however, he had discovered through studying the scriptures that purple was more than the color worn by the Lakers and the Ravens. It was a color of royalty. Kings wore purple, and Jamal felt like a king.

"You know what? I've been down, like, four flat tires for these past couple of months, but now I got my swagger back," Quincy reported as he checked himself out in the mirror and adjusted his tie.

"We all got our swagger turned way up." Will inserted his handkerchief into his front pocket.

"Some more than other," Quincy noted, referring to Chauncey, who was having difficulty with his handkerchief.

Jamal found delight at the sight of Will in a suit. Will had made a complete transformation from a skilled car thief to a fierce warrior for God. Jamal admired Will for his courage to change his life in spite of his obstacles.

"I see you, Will," Jamal said.

"Oh, you know, I can't wear a ProClub T-shirt and khakis on my boy's big day."

"Cherese is looking good. You been seeing a lot of each other lately," Jamal said.

"Yeah, you know we're trying to take it slow, but she's real cool," Will said.

"I can't wait until I get married." Chauncey put on his jacket.

"We can't, either," Quincy said. "I'll be glad when you can experience the fourth heaven so you can loosen up," he added to the chuckles of Jamal and Will.

"You know what, Brother Page? I spend hours praying for you to get right. I know you're a Christian, but you got some ways about you," Chauncey said.

"I love you too!" Quincy said, and everyone laughed.

"I love you too," Chauncey said and shook his head.

*Love* was not a word that Jamal uttered to other men, but Jamal loved his brothers like King David loved Jonathan. "Hey, I love you guys. I wouldn't be who I am today if it weren't for you guys."

Titus entered the dressing room in a white robe, with a kente cloth draped around his shoulders. "Okay, game on. Let's do this."

The moment had arrived, and butterflies had a meeting in the pit of Jamal's stomach. He would be a husband, and finally, he would be a father to Jamir. Jamal followed Titus out of the dressing room and down the hall. His knees felt a little weak, but he refused to stumble while walking to the altar. Instead, he thought about his president and tried to adopt the swagger walk that President Obama used.

"What's wrong with your walk?" Quincy said.

"Nothing." Jamal looked back and laughed, slight embarrassed.

The sanctuary had been transformed with white flowers and purple ribbons. Young and old, family and friends were in attendance. Jamal walked along the side of the sanctuary, with his brothers behind him, as he made his way to the front of the altar.

After a few minutes at the altar, Jamal wanted to pass out if he had to stand there any longer. The mixture of excitement and anxiety made the room spin. A pat on the back from Quincy stopped the spinning, and Jamal returned to relaxed mode. The musicians started to play Eric Benét and Tamia's duet "Spend My Life With You."

Jamir came out first as the ring bearer. Only three years old, he walked down the aisle by himself and stole everyone's hearts. Jamal gave his son a kiss on the forehead when Jamir made his way to the aisle and stood in front of him. Next, the flower girls made their way down to the altar, tossing purple and white petals on the floor.

Jamal had three best men, because there was no way he could rank the importance of each man in his life. Quincy was Jamal's ideal of success, and he had helped Jamal to exude excellence in every area of his life. Chauncey's faith was strong enough to guide anyone through turbulent times, and Will was the most genuine person Jamal had ever met.

Groomsmen in black suits and bridesmaids in purple gowns swayed to the music as they made their way down to the altar and positioned themselves alongside the bride and alongside the groom. The ushers closed the doors, the music stopped, and then the longest moment passed before the sanctuary doors reopened. The music began playing again, which meant one thing: Chantel was prepared to make her way down the aisle. She had on a white veil and a smile that could be seen from a distance through the veil. Every doubt had been wiped from Jamal's mind, and he saw the one woman who understood him the best come down the aisle.

She walked down the aisle by herself. For years Chantel had been estranged from her family, and she had not grown up with a sense of family and unconditional love. That all would come to an end today. Jamal and Jamir would love her unconditionally, and Jamal would be her hero, and Jesus would be her Savior.

When Chantel was close enough, Jamal took her by both hands, and the two faced each other. The warmth of Chantel's hands quickened Jamal's heart as if it were the first time he had touched her.

"Let us pray." Titus placed his hands on Jamal's and Chantel's shoulders." Lord, we come to you to celebrate the union of this couple. As they make a commitment both to each other and to you, I pray that we are all reminded of the commitment we have made both to you and to each other. Amen."

"You're beautiful," Jamal whispered to Chantel.

Chantel flashed a big smile, and Jamal could barely contain his desire to kiss her and place everything at his wife's feet.

"Marriage carries such significance that when Jesus was on the earth, he attended a wedding. So therefore marriage is not a simple union between man and woman, but a commitment that involves man, woman, and God." Titus turned toward Jamal. "Jamal, do you take Chantel as your wife?"

"I do." Jamal let a chuckle slip, because he was certain that there would be days when he wished he didn't.

"And, Chantel, do you take Jamal as your husband?"

"I do," an ecstatic Chantel said.

The ceremony was traditional, but Chantel and Jamal had decided to take communion together. With each vow exchanged, Jamal knew he was ready to go the distance with her.

"You may kiss the bride," Titus said.

Jamal kissed Chantel, and though it wasn't the first time he had kissed her, it was the first time he had kissed her as his wife, and that distinction alone was special.

"Ladies and gentlemen, I present to you Mr. and Mrs. Jamal Taylor," the DJ announced over the microphone in the grand ballroom of the Carson community center.

Jamal and Chantel walked out into a ballroom filled with family, friends, and members of the church. Jamal was amazed at how many people had chosen to spend their New Year's Eve celebrating his and Chantel's vows. The year had been filled with highs and lows for Jamal, but this night nullified all the lows.

The ballroom was decorated in Jamal and Chantel's wedding colors. Some guests dined on a simple meal of herbed chicken and red potatoes, while everyone else danced, as they had come to party.

"I love you," Chantel uttered into Jamal's ear over the boisterous music.

"I love you too." Jamal snuck a kiss before Chantel could respond.

"I want to dance." Chantel stood up in her form-fitting white gown.

"Man, I'm retired. I get out on the dance floor and I might hurt myself." Jamal took a sip of his iced tea.

"Come on, old man." Chantel took Jamal by the hand.

Jamal and Chantel made their way to the dance floor. They danced to a song from the new jack swing era. Jamal and Chantel laughed they performed popular dances from the early nineties. Then the music changed to a modern song, and the younger people got on the dance floor and started dancing.

"We're not about to let them outdo us," Chantel said to Jamal.

Chantel started to dance as best she could in her dress, while Jamal danced his way to exhaustion. The young adults responded by dancing more energetically, and a battle ensued, with Jamal and Chantel gracefully bowing out to the more vigorous group.

"We're going to party like this for the rest of our lives," Chantel shouted over the loud music as the DJ switched to a slower tempo song and more people started to dance.

"With God's blessing," Jamal said.

"Congrats," Chauncey said as he and Rachel danced around them.

"You're next," Jamal said.

Quincy and Karen danced and exchanged laughs. Even Will managed to get out on the dance floor and allow Cherese, the young lady he met in Palm Springs—and who, it turned out, lived in Los Angeles—to guide him through a dance. The four brothers of God were still intact. Jamal had vowed to be a good father to Jamir, a good husband to Chantel, and a great friend to his brothers.

# Epilogue

Will became fidgety as the line stood still for several minutes. He preferred a nice evening instead of this cattle call of an environment.

"I told you we should've gone to the one in Gardena," Odell said as he looked on.

"The one in Gardena is usually busy as well," Cherese said.

"I'm saying, though, in a minute I'm going to cut out of line and get my own plate," Odell said.

"Dad, be cool. We're going to eat soon enough," Will remarked.

"Man, I'm about to get it in." Joshua rubbed his stomach.

Carroll was too wrapped up in a game of peekaboo with Elisha to worry about how slowly the line moved. Will had noticed that he had passed at least three Home Town Buffets before the family decided to come to the one in Hawthorne.

"My bad on the wait, but this one is supposed to be really good," Will said to Cherese.

"I'm not tripping. It's okay." Cherese flashed Will her award-winning smile.

"I am. These people are playing with me, walking around with their salads and chicken, teasing me," Odell said.

They arrived at the front of the line just when Will's father was about to go off. Will paid for the entire family with his debit card and followed Cherese through the salad bar. Cherese was a down chick, and Will loved that about her. Moments later, Will and Cherese made it to the table where Odell, Carroll, Elisha, and Joshua sat with plates of food.

"Like I said, bro, we're about to get it in," Joshua said, rubbing his hands together in anticipation of his first bite.

"But first . . ." Will took Cherese and Joshua by the hands. Odell and Carroll joined in, and even Elisha, with her petite hand, held on to his mother's hand. "Thank you, Father, for family and for your grace, which sustains. Bless this food, and bless those who prepared it. In Jesus's name, amen!"

They ate as a family, with Cherese giving Joshua firm smacks on the hand whenever he tried to reach over to her plate.


"Please, Lord, let it be a boy. Please, Lord." Quincy could not recall the last time he had prayed so hard. He suspected it might have been when the Cowboys were in the Super Bowl.

"Relax, Q," Jamal said as he patted his friend's shoulder in the waiting room.

"I can't relax, and where is this fool at?" Quincy groaned, referring to Dwight, who had vowed to be there at his child's birth.

"He'll be here," Chauncey said as he put away his magazine.

Karen came in, frantic. "The baby is crowning. Where is he?"

"I don't know, but I'm here." Quincy stood up and made his way toward the door.

Just as Quincy reached the door, Dwight ran in.

"I'm here, Mr. Page. I'm sorry I'm late, but—"

"Save it, and get in there." Quincy turned Dwight around and ushered him to the door.

"I told you," Chauncey said.

"Yeah, you were right. Now, all I need is for my grandchild to be a boy, and I'll be happy. I can't handle another girl in my life."

"Whatever is the case, we're here for you," Jamal said.

Moments later Karen emerged with a smile on her face. "Your daughter gave birth to a healthy baby girl." Karen embraced a stunned Quincy.

"I figured that. Congrats, Brother Page." Chauncey patted Quincy on the back.

Jamal was smart enough to keep his distance, because Quincy proceeded to haul off and smack Chauncey upside the head.

"Go look." Karen pointed toward the delivery room.

Quincy took slow steps toward the delivery room. He tried to catch his breath, for once he saw his granddaughter, his nightmare would become an official reality. Quincy entered the delivery room and walked around a curtain that shielded his daughter. Nurses were working to clean up the area, and Dwight stood over a physically worn Sasha. Dwight looked like a proud father, and Sasha had a maternal glow that superseded the sweat and tears in her eyes.

"Dad, come on and meet your granddaughter," Sasha said as cradled the baby in her arms.

Quincy got close enough to give Dwight a handshake and take a look at his grandbaby. Her eyes stole Quincy's heart. It was like he had witnessed the birth of Sasha all over again.

"We named her Faith." Sasha extended the tiny baby to Quincy.

Quincy held Faith in his hands as she fussed and cried.

"Faith! That's all right!" Quincy said as he pondered how faith and love went hand in hand.

# Readers' Questions

1. In *The Retreat 2* Chauncey tries to find love through the Internet. Is online dating an appropriate venue for Christians to meet?

2. In *The Retreat 2* Jamal and Chantel live together for a while. Can a couple live together before marriage and resist temptation?

3. Quincy has to deal with his daughter being pregnant. What degree of responsibility does he and Karen have with respect to Sasha's decisions?

4. Is Will too judgmental toward his parents?

5. In *The Retreat 2* Jamal and Chantel attend premarital counseling. Is premarital counseling necessary in this day and age?

6. Chauncey falls for Rachel, a nonbeliever. Can a believer and a nonbeliever have a successful relationship?

7. Should Quincy continue to support and financially back Sasha?

8. Is Pastor Titus Dawkins in the right when he confronts the women of the church?

9. Which character do you feel grew the most by the end of *The Retreat 2*?

10. Would you want to see a third *Retreat*?

# UC HIS GLORY BOOK CLUB!

## *www.uchisglorybookclub.net*

UC His Glory Book Club is the spirit-inspired brain-child of Joylynn Jossel, an author and acquisitions editor of Urban Christian, and Kendra Norman-Bellamy, an author for Urban Christian. This is an online book club that hosts authors of Urban Christian. We welcome as members all men and women who have a passion for reading Christian-based fiction.

UC His Glory Book Club pledges its commitment to provide support, positive feedback, encouragement, and a forum whereby members can openly discuss and review the literary works of Urban Christian authors.

There is no membership fee associated with UC His Glory Book Club; however, we do ask that you support the authors through book purchases, encouragement, book reviews and, of course, your prayers. We also ask that you respect our beliefs and follow the guidelines of the book club. We hope to receive your valuable input, your opinions, and reviews that build up, rather than tear down, our authors.

# What We Believe:

—We believe that Jesus is the Christ, Son of the Living God.

—We believe the Bible is the true, living Word of God.

—We believe all Urban Christian authors should use their God-given writing abilities to honor God and to share the message of the written word God has given to each of them uniquely.

—We believe in supporting Urban Christian authors in their literary endeavors by reading, purchasing, and sharing their titles with our online community.

—We believe that everything we do in our literary arena should be done in a manner that will lead to God being glorified and honored.

We look forward to the online fellowship with you. Please visit us often at *www.uchisglorybookclub.net*.

Many Blessing to You!

Shelia E. Lipsey,
President, UC His Glory Book Club